TO CLAIM A PRINCE

THE PRINCE SAGA: BOOK 1

S.NASONOV

Dedications

To Molly, for being there in the beginning.

To my ladies on Tik Tok, you know who you are.

CHAPTER 1

NON-CONTRARY MARY

"Excellent news, Mary!" a boisterous male voice echoed off the walls of the indoor playground. Mary looked up from the padded triangle she had been rigorously wiping to see her boss' panting frame. His cheeks were ruddy and brow was damp with excitement (or perhaps he had taken the stairs? Good for him).

Mary liked Mr. Malinowski, he was kind and fair and paid her slightly above minimum wage.

His round glasses matched a round phy-
sique, an upturned mustache wriggling as
he spoke.

It reminded her of those hairy caterpillars
she never allowed herself to touch. A girl in
fifth grade had told her that those hairs contained poison so Mary came to the conclusion it was safer to skip caterpillar touching.

Mr. M's mustache probably wasn't coated in
poison, but Mary was equally as dissuaded
from touching it.

"My sweet Esmeralda convinced her sister,
you know the one who manages the library,
to let us run an informational booth."

Mary did not personally know Esmeralda
or her library managing sister, but felt like
it was not appropriate to mention it at that
moment. Mr. M frequently prattled on about
one problem or another, and Mary was always happy to listen.

She rested the damp silver-impregnated rag

on the padded mat, anticipating the length of this particular tangent may exceed her cleaning stamina.

She was also just glad to be rid of it, the texture of the microfiber cloth made her palms itch—if Mary was in charge she would outlaw microfiber outright—but she was not the boss, and inventory management was well above her pay grade.

How does one decide on the optimal cleaning cloth, anyway?

Was there some standardized wiping efficiency scale out there?

Mary would have to look it up later, after she dealt with whatever her boss wanted. It must be important because he looked at her with excited expectation.

Had he said something she was supposed to respond to?

Mr. M didn't hire her for stellar intellect or

exceptional skill—Mary was well aware her main positive attribute was unconditional tolerance. She was completely unphased by emotional outbursts or temper tantrums (a useful trait when one was forced to interact with toddlers and their parents).

Useful for interacting with Mr. M as well, all things considered.

Although her official role was only to sanitize play equipment and set up for birthday parties, she often found herself being a confidant to those around her.

This job had taught Mary many things, some more useful than others.

She was exceptionally good at spotting hand foot and mouth disease on sticky toddler fingers, and could unwrap a cheese string in less than five seconds. Some may see those skills as insignificant, but Mary chose to view them as her strengths.

Unfortunately, she was also prone to a wandering mind. It was the familiar equilibrium of every report card she has received in childhood: 'Has great potential, poor follow-through.'

Mr. M cleared his throat, waiting for Mary to inquire further about his latest venture.

"An informational booth," she repeated, brain trying to make the connection that would justify Mr. M's excitement.

Was there another measles outbreak?

That kid yesterday looked a bit rashy. Mary should have said something—she took the safety of the other children very seriously.

The indoor play area was situated in a rather affluent neighborhood, meaning the vaccination rates were likely too low for herd immunity. It made Mary snort that rich people thought they were impervious to infectious diseases.

Perhaps if they invented an organic, gluten-free, dairy-free, big pharma free variety the odds would be better. On second thought, vaccines are likely already gluten-free.

Rich people always made Mary nervous—she was constantly anticipating the moment she would say something to offend them.

"Precisely," Mr. M confirmed, finger lifting in the air.

Mary hummed and nodded, attempting to sound interested.

Truthfully, she didn't care about whatever the portly man was scheming, but she had a feeling it directly implicated her.

"The topic is relevant, prudent, and most importantly, life saving." The man gesticulated wildly with his puffy hands, a sheen of excitement on his face.

Mary wasn't keen to believe him, considering he thought silver weaved rags were adequately antibacterial. Regardless, she nodded and continued to wipe, picturing the armies of tiny microbes dueling on a battlefield of microfiber.

"Well, don't you want to know the details?" he asked, tone now tinged with impatience. Mary sat up and placed the rag and spray bottle on her lap, demonstrating rapt attention.

"Yes, of course, please tell me." she smiled and nodded politely, kicking herself internally for making him feel like she wasn't interested—nobody deserved to feel invisible.

"Carbon monoxide poisoning!" he exploded, flaying his fingers out in what she would consider jazz hands.

Mary's mouth popped open, heart suddenly hammering with panic. Mr. M took her momentary shock as an invitation to keep speaking.

"After we lost our darling Ronald last September I fell into a deep and crippling depression. Cheryl—you know with the large hair and small lips—" Mary recalled that was his grief counselor. "She mentioned that action may be a more constructive way to process my grief as opposed to weeping incessantly."

Mary remembered that Ronald was Mr. M's elderly Pomeranian. They found him unresponsive in the garage a few months prior, with no official cause of death (he did not want to 'disgrace Ronald's resting spirit' by having a necropsy done). Mr. M subsequently became obsessed with the possibility that a carbon monoxide leak was the cause, after seeing a PSA during the commercial break of his soap opera.

As he rambled, Mary couldn't help imagining Ronald attaching a dog sized hose to a dog sized tail pipe.

Perhaps he'd had a mental breakdown from being separated from his food dish?

CHAPTER 1

Mary suspected obesity was the likely culprit of his sudden demise, as Ronald looked more like a sausage with legs than a dog. Nevertheless, clearly this was important to Mr. Malinowski, so it should be important to Mary as well.

"I didn't know you moonlight as a safety educator," she said, surprised he'd never mentioned it before—the man shared most of his thoughts, feelings, and bodily functions. Mary stood, tucking the bottle and rag into the pit of her arm.

"I don't," he said gripping her shoulders warmly, "But I do know a beautiful, smart, and obedient young employee who would be willing to share this important and life saving information." She felt his grip intensify when he spoke of her obedience, as if needing to remind her.

She shook off his hold gently, understanding finally seeping into the folds of her brain.

Considering Mary was short and stout with

plain features, Mr. M was obviously trying to use flattery to grease her into agreeing. She didn't typically require much coercion, being helpful was one of the only things she was good at.

She was, however, petrified at the idea of being so exposed.

"I'm not sure I would do a great job. I don't know anything about carbon monoxide or its hazards," she said tentatively, walking over to the storage closet and placing the cleaning supplies on the shelf. Mr. M waddled behind her, close on her heels.

"Yes, but even if one life is saved my heart can rebuild." He held his chest emphatically. "Besides, it'll all be in the pamphlet. All you have to do is stand there and look approachable."

Easier said than done.

Mary didn't consider herself particularly approachable, her mother always chastised her for scrunching her eyebrows together when she wasn't paying attention.

She tried to put on a charismatic front, especially when she was tasked with doing things she wasn't interested in, as if plastering a smile to her face would manifest the destruction of the gnawing anxiety that followed her.

Mary suspected that sweet Esmeralda had something to do with this bizarre idea. Last week Mr. M mentioned his wife had to put an ointment on his face twice a day for 'tear-related dermatitis'.

She could imagine that caring for the dramatic man would be laborious and exhausting. It seemed like a very reasonable trade— Mary's lone suffering in exchange for the survival of Mr. M's whole family.

She had to do this; if she didn't he could fly off the handle, get a messy and expensive divorce, be forced to sell his business, and she would be left unemployed.

Mary could do this. For Esmeralda.

"Alright," she agreed, giving him the warmest smile she could muster.

CHAPTER 2
COLOURLESS AND ODORLESS

Mr. Malinowski clearly overestimated the thirst of the general public for carbon monoxide safety awareness. She was only one hour into her booth duty and it was looking grim.

Mary did her best—the smile she plastered on her face was large if not a little forced. She made a solid attempt to find answers to questions she was wildly unprepared for, to not fail miserably and disappointed her boss.

"Does it smell that bad?" a teenage boy asked, his frame was made up of mostly curly hair and hoodie. Despite the barrier of teenage angst, she could still see the look of disgust on his face.

"Oh, um, it's odourless actually, it just occupies the place in your lungs where oxygen should be." Mary had done a small amount of research the night before, so she was confident on the basics.

In highschool she had discovered that her performance anxiety had a very simple exploit: Purpose—if she had a job to do, the spotlight didn't threaten to burn her alive.

They wouldn't be judging her as a person, only the information she was communicating. It was an important mind trick that made the panic of being seen recede.

Most of the time.

She placed her shaking palms behind her, hoping the boy couldn't smell her fear. He scoffed and walked off, allowing Mary to release the breath she was holding.

Although her nerves were fried, she was grateful someone talked to her at all—a small group of tween girls just pointed and laughed when she was setting up the display.

Hours passed and her stack of pamphlets remained untouched.

Disappointment began to build in Mary's chest; not one person had scanned the QR code on her shirt. Fortunately, she did exhaust the supply of stickers after the first Mommy-and-me story time class, but she was skeptical that toddlers were the target population to begin with.

Mary thought it was bizarre to have a reading class for babies since she was almost certain they couldn't read.

"Um, excuse me, miss. Your fart cloud is falling down," a gentle male voice interrupted her mounting despair.

Mary looked up to see a young, well dressed man pointing towards the top portion of her booth.

She stuck her head out and partially climbed onto the plastic surface, trying to understand what he was talking about.

Her stomach dropped when she absorbed the sight in front of her.

The green plywood cloud cut out that was hanging above her really did resemble a cartoon fart. It certainly didn't help that the banner had 'Silent and Deadly' in large bubble letters.

The graphic was listing dramatically to one side, hanging on for dear life.

Mary suddenly felt the need to hold on to something as well, flooding horror making her head spin.

She assumed it was meant to represent carbon monoxide gas, which was both factually incorrect and artistically bankrupt.

Mary threw her head back and groaned. No wonder nobody was seriously interested in her message –it appeared she was educating on the dangers of errant flatulence.

Her misery was interrupted when the slippery pamphlets beneath her palm shifted and tumbled towards the gray carpet.

Mary should have been concerned about the fact this caused her side to slam down painfully on the booth table, but the only thing that wounded her was the loud sound and paper mess she made with her clumsiness.

"Oh, god, are you okay?" the man asked, reaching his hand out to help her up. He was an average height for a man, definitely under six feet but not by much. He could have been taller but there was a significant hunch to his posture, like he wasn't comfortable taking up space.

It made her sad for the stranger, he was quite slim so she couldn't imagine he took up much space.

Following Archimedes' principle, he wouldn't displace many of the molecules around him (if he was sitting in a bath the water would doubtfully rise more than a few inches).

His long spindly legs would probably hang out of Mary's small tub, though.

She was grateful she had a tub at all, considering how little rent she paid. Her apartment was a run down little studio—working part time at a children's playground didn't afford her a luxurious life. No, this man would likely need to have a shower if he came over.

Mary shook her head to clear the image of this stranger bathing in her apartment.

His fingers were cool against hers as she swiveled herself to a seated position, legs hanging over the front edge of the booth.

A warm tingle remained when he let go of her hand, a stark contrast to the comforting cadence of his voice.

Face flushing with embarrassment, Mary trained her gaze down towards the pile of pamphlets on the ground. They lay discarded and disgraced, closely mirroring her professional integrity.

"I got it," the man said before she could hop down to grab them.

He dropped to his knees, and the world slowed.

Mary's breath caught as she admired the planes of his back, the tight muscled ridges of his trapezius was visible through the white linen of a completely un-wrinkled dress shirt. She had the unexplainable urge to dig her fingers into the straining flesh, to make him groan in relief.

The wave of arousal was hot and unexpected, a flash fire through the temperate rainforest that was her libido.

It was as if all of the hydrogen bonds in the room had broken, leaving not one spec of usable air. He neatly and efficiently collected the sheets of glossy paper, finally raising his gaze to hers and holding up the tidy pile of pamphlets.

He looked like a prince.

Not classically handsome, his face was largely overpowered by a nose which had a noticeable bump in the center. Mary wondered whether it was a natural deformity or if he had broken it in the past.

Would that make him sexier?

Her mother would frequently make vulgar remarks about the stars of action films, especially when they were half naked and covered in the blood of their enemies. Mary never really understood the appeal, but to each their own.

She preferred nice men that could hold a decent conversation more than anything. This man certainly didn't look like he was brimming with uncontrolled testosterone.

He was pale, with a smattering of purple under his eyes that juxtaposed a dark lock of hair that must have fallen from its tidy styled home on the top of his head.

Mary allowed a split second of delusion that he was on his knees for her, a knight who showed up to save her from the misery of educating the public.

No, he was not especially beautiful.

To her, he was perfect.

"Oh, um, thank you." she finally spoke, her higher brain function returning.

A flash of fear filled blue irises and his gaze was gone, breaking the mesmerizing connection. He nodded, grabbed a pamphlet, and walked away.

Her prince was a skittish one.

Mary watched the mysterious man as he walked and sat at one of the tables at the back, squarely between the mystery and fantasy sections.

He was a mysterious fantasy, indeed.

His movements were awkward and lethargic as he pulled out a novel from his bag. The distance allowed her to scan his frame, pleased to see that he was wearing stereotypical business attire.

Mary's chest tingled (she always appreciated a man that was employed). However, as usual, guilt followed like a rabies-affected stray dog—the man was clearly ill and/or exhausted and she let him pick up the mess she made.

CHAPTER 2

She had to find a way to repay him for his kindness.

The rest of Mary's shift was uneventful, mostly due to the fact that her focus was on the sickly man at the back of the room, her mind constantly replaying the short interaction and every mistake she made.

She watched him out of the corner of her eye for the entire hour he read, trying not to linger on the bulge of his Adam's apple when he swallowed the saliva that must have been collecting in his mouth.

She absolutely was not interested in his mouth, no matter how pouty and full his lips were.

Mary shook her head, a sad attempt to clear away lustful thoughts. He was probably an asshole, anyway, not worth wasting a crush on. Satisfied with her rationale, she returned to repeatedly shifting the unused materials splayed out in front of her, and definitely not thinking about the way he would whimper if she replaced the book in front of him with her pussy.

Her hand froze on one of the decorative buttons she was polishing when he stood, tucked the book into his laptop bag and stepped towards the exit.

Just before he passed the booth, the same piercing blues met hers once again, this time a hint of a smile softening his gaze.

"It was nice to meet you," they said, before disappearing through automatic glass doors.

Adrenaline made mush of Mary's muscles, a weight slowly crushing her chest.

She desperately needed an orgasm.

Or a lobotomy.

CHAPTER 2

Her work schedule returned to usual, early mornings three times a week.

Mary found her thoughts lingering on the lonesome stranger as she wiped a suspiciously urine-coloured puddle from underneath the miniature trampoline.

Did he come to the library regularly?

What did he do there?

Mary had many challenges—impulse control was one of them.

This fascination was completely out of character for her. She was usually a good level-headed girl; she went to work everyday and did her job to her best ability and she did not become infatuated with the first stranger that got down on his knees for her.

Mary began to doubt if he actually got down on his knees for her at all.

Technically, he knelt down to clean up her mess, which was just as novel. She wasn't used to having anyone clean up her messes. It was usually the other way around, as evidenced by the suspicious brown smudge that was left on the disturbing microfiber cloth. There was no way that man would ever actually demean himself for her, not in the way her deviant mind suddenly materialized.

The prospect of her new obsession kneeling for her on purpose was too salacious to be believed.

Besides, if he was interested he would have talked to her (men were not shy in their advances, from her experience).

However, the concept of a submissive man was not completely foreign to her—one of her previous boyfriends had enjoyed being pegged. It didn't particularly arouse Mary but she was a pretty tolerant person and had a hard time rejecting people.

One time she jokingly asked a man to beg for her cunt and he laughed just at the suggestion. That rejection felt like a very large and hot knife in her chest and she would rather swallow an entire clutch of spider eggs than make anyone feel that way.

Mary was comfortable with her role as the happy recipient of romantic intentions. It was easy and simple and nobody got hurt that way, especially not her.

So, why couldn't she get the idea of that helpful man worshiping her out of her mind?

"Mary, darling," Mr. M crept up behind her, almost startling the apple sauce pouch right out of her hand. "How did it go?" he inquired, hands clutching the lapels of a crushed velvet blazer.

Mary swallowed. She didn't want to upset him with the truth of her failure—she'd prefer to stop thinking about it altogether.

"There were some technical difficulties, but we really cracked the infant demographic I think." She shut the fridge door and turned to face her boss.

Instead of gratitude his mustached face sported disappointment.

A painful cramp gripped Mary's stomach.

One of Mary's other flaws was inability to take criticism. Well, she could take it but she would be crying about it in the supply closet later.

"About that..." Mr. M began, lips pressed together in pity. Mary steeled herself, ready for her rightful termination.

"I'm sorry," she apologized, unable to stop herself. Perhaps she could salvage the situation with enough begging and logical explanation. "The fart cloud was falling down, and I slipped on the pamphlets—the paper was of a very high quality, too glossy in fact. It was bad. No, I mean I was bad-" Her words came out in a flurry, breaths fast and shallow.

"Mary," Mr. M grabbed her by the shoulders and shook vigorously. "Snap out of it."

"Sorry, please continue."

"This is precisely what I wanted to speak to you about," he began, turning and sashaying towards the break room. Mary followed behind him, heart hammering in time with his speedy gallop.

"I'll be the first to admit that I haven't been the best employer." He pulled out a rusted foldable chair for her before sitting on his own.

"No, don't say that-" she began but Mr. M held up his hand to stop her.

"I've been working you too hard. Look at you, you're a nervous wreck." He gestured towards her. Truthfully, Mary hadn't been nervous at all until he started this conversation. The older man sighed, a sympathetic look in his eyes.

"You're going on vacation."

Mary blinked.

"No, I'm not?" Her words sounded more like a question, despite the fact that she was very certain she had no trip planned.

Mary had never been on a vacation as an

adult. Her father had taken her to Disne-yLand as a child, but he was so absorbed with his work phone she was basically alone.

She did enjoy the churros, though.

Mr. M nodded somberly. "Yes, you are. You have been an adequate employee for near-ly seven years and I feel an obligation for your physical and mental health. You are going off for a week on compassionate leave." He scooped her hands into his big meaty paws, a clear attempt at empathy.

"Compassionate leave? Who needs the compassion?" Mary couldn't stop the con-fusion from slipping onto her face. She didn't have any dying family members as far as she could remember.

"You," he said, "from me." Mr. M placed a gentle kiss on the back of her hand, making Mary withdraw her palms from his weird-ly affectionate grip.

She wasn't sure what was going on with her boss, but decided she probably didn't want to know.

"It may be unpaid, but I am sure the rest will be revitalizing." he said, standing abruptly and turning to leave the pathetic excuse for a break room.

"Besides, it's important to do something nice for yourself."

CHAPTER 3

AN UNCONVENTION-AL ALIBI

Mary visited the library every day of her forced vacation. She told herself it was the most economically sound decision, but in reality, she was hoping to see her handsome stranger again.

She puttered around her miniscule apartment for the entire morning before she found herself getting on the bus. She had washed, dried, and folded every article of clothing she owned, vacuumed, mopped, and dusted every available surface and still had several hours left before lunch.

The entire time she worked her boss' words rang in her mind like the gong before a martial arts match, not that she had ever participated in a competitive sport.

"Do something nice for yourself," she grumbled, aggressively scrubbing the grout of her kitchen floor. Her mother always said the nicest thing anyone could do for themselves was to get their life together.

Mary's life was together enough, wasn't it?

So what if she had no love, friendship, money, status, or power?

She had integrity and discipline, and that was more important than self-indulgence. Selfish people were hurtful, and that was the opposite of what she wanted.

When her back was too sore to continue, Mary took a break.

She had made an attempt to read but found her mind wandering off of the ink on the page and back to the mysterious stranger from the library.

Perhaps she just needed a more interesting book, something so salacious it would distract her mind from edging towards obsession.

Yes, that was a very good honorable reason to visit the library. It had nothing to do with the bolt of excitement that ran through her at the thought of seeing him again.

The ache of disappointment lingered in her chest as she browsed the shelves leisurely. Of course he wouldn't be there during the day, most people worked during business hours.

Unless he had a sexy nighttime job. That would explain how exhausted he looked. Mary bit her lip as she considered what deviant professions her muse could have.

Unfortunately, that line of thinking didn't yield many results, considering he looked more like a night auditor than a stripper or escort.

A wave of arousal seeped between her thighs when she imagined leaning over the counter of a fancy hotel and pulling him closer by the tie around his neck. His blue eyes would flash with fear again, followed by a quiet desire.

Would he be too shy to throw her down on the counter and ravage her?

It was hard to fantasize about a man she knew nothing about. Some women could insert their crush into a daydream of their wishing, but Mary didn't feel right even imagining the man do something he didn't want to do. She took consent very seriously, and there was nothing sexier than a man losing his mind with desire.

No, she couldn't truly fantasize about him until she got a better sense of his character.

As if called by her naughty thoughts, the

mystery man walked through the glass doors and towards the same table as the day before.

A creature of habit.

Mary quickly ducked behind a row of books, watching him through a small slit between the covers.

Looking at him in secret felt sensual, voyeuristic.

He was on display for her while she was hidden, safe from his judgment. No one would know about her lapse in morality.

His frame was still clad with the same white button down, dress pants and brown leather shoes as the previous day. He still looked like he didn't quite eat enough or get enough sleep, and Mary had the sudden and uncontrollable urge to feed him and tuck him into bed, and not in the fun sexy way.

Well, maybe after.

Mary didn't know much, but she knew that staring at a stranger was creepy behavior. She couldn't go to the library just to watch at a possibly ill, unconventionally handsome man.

No, she needed to create plausible deniability of her deranged fascination.

Mary took the necessary precautions; she continued to wear her "Say NO to CO!" shirt, to create an alibi for her likely future arrest.

No officer, this man simply looked so sickly he needed her close supervision.

Yes, she was an expert as per her shirt, and he was free to scan the QR code for more information.

Yes, she was aware that carbon monoxide is both colorless and odorless and her shirt was a personal insult to the field of chemistry.

To add to her alibi, Mary figured she should

look like she was doing something normal and not stalker-like. She sat a reasonable distance away from him and began to scribble in a spare notebook she kept in her backpack, the princely stranger on her mind.

Her mother gifted her the book to fill with her hopes and dreams when she couldn't come up with anything for her career planning class in high school, and it had stayed completely blank (though she did pass the class).

Though it likely would horrify her mother to discover what she planned to use it for, she supposed writing down her most depraved fantasies would meet the technicality of 'hopes and dreams'.

She allowed herself to glance at him after every paragraph, carefully not to arouse too much suspicion.

Excitement throbbed inside her—this game fueled a fire in her loins that she never knew existed. Mary began to imagine that a man like that could look at her, could want her.

Who would she need to be in order to deserve complete devotion?

Her mind reeled with the delusion of arousal, longing to feel the heat of sensual power.

Mistress sat at the vanity, the bristles of an aged hairbrush pressing into her scalp. A soft knock at the door startled her, making a brown lock jump from its place on her chest. The heartbeat beneath it began to race just knowing he was near. She stood slowly, measured steps instilling the unwavering control she tried desperately to exude.

The Prince must wait for her.

Despite her best efforts, the doorknob quivered in her grasp, the skin of her hands slick with anxiety.

The lustful looks he gave her from his seat at the grand dining table still lingered behind her eyelids as she attempted to take a long grounding breath, simultaneously attempting to dispel the whisper of his touch from the sensitive skin behind her knee. His actions as she served his dinner were not missed, and there would be consequences.

Taking one last steadying breath, Mistress pulled open the door.

She knew what her Prince looked like, could have described him easily to any travelling artist or vendor at the fair.

Golden hair, blue eyes, strong cheekbones and full lips.

Other characteristics belonged only to her—the mischief currently twinkling in those eyes being her most treasured. The world knew him as the heir to the throne, a responsible, capable, if not slightly privileged and arrogant man.

She knew him in a completely different way altogether.

"Good evening, Mistress. May I come in?" His lithe frame stood comfortably in the doorway, as if this too belonged to him.

Mistress took a deep breath.

"I'm not sure that is appropriate, your majesty—visiting a common girl's private quarters," she said, stepping aside so he could enter the room. He looked opulent surrounded by the blandness of the decor, the gold trim and satin finishes of his clothes stark against the worn wood.

He was handsome and regal, a diamond amongst river stones.

"I don't know what common girl you speak of, I only see a goddess." His tone was casual but his gaze was heated. Before Mistress could respond the Prince grabbed the back of her head and slammed their mouths together, pressing her up against the door.

Their tongues tangled deeply, bodies pressed close.

"My siren calls me with her full lips and plentiful curves. She beckons me closer with her coy smiles and I am lost to her," he moaned, peppering her neck and chest with kisses. His hands shifted to knead her rear underneath the cotton slip, causing the woman to arch her back. She clutched the back of the Prince's head, threading calloused fingers into the silky strands of his hair and pulling back sharply.

She could not let him win.

"I am no siren, but you are most definitely lost. A Prince who is wandering, hoping for a release inside a girl of no notice," she hissed, nipping at his ear lobe while keeping his head immobilized in her grip. Heat flooded her core at his answering moan. "A woman who could be discarded."

"No," he growled and pulled out of grasp, a rush of air cooling her damp skin.

"I am a man who is desperate for you. What must I do to convince you of my intentions?" His chest laboured with breath, the wildness in his eyes and flush to his cheeks sprouting satisfaction in Mistress' chest. She could see the obvious tenting of his trousers, indicating his physical need for her.

How could the Prince show her she

was more than a frivolous conquest?

"On your knees."

A sudden throb between her legs pulled Mary from her fantasy. She didn't expect to have such a physical reaction to the Prince's devotion. She glanced up at her muse who was reading peacefully, face concentrated as usual.

Would Mary like the real prince to kneel for her?

What if he saw her as the Prince saw his Mistress?

The Prince dropped to his knees, needy eyes locked to his Mistress.

"If I order you to pleasure me with your mouth, will you obey? Will you still spend your time with me if I said you will not be getting your own release?" Mistress stepped forward, pressing the front of her legs to his groin and tenderly running her fingers through his hair.

The Prince closed his eyes for a moment, relishing in her touch.

"It would be an honor, my goddess," he purred, taking one delicate palm and trailing it up from her ankle, raising the shift up with it. The fabric folded as it moved, a curtain unveiling the opening act of a sensual opera. His eyes never left hers, the heat in them fueling Mistress' desire.

His mouth pressed to her sex and her body began to sing.

Mary shut the notebook forcefully, causing nearby patrons to glance her way, including the prince. The skin of her cheeks heated, matching the unbearable scorch in her core, arousal pulsing at the thought of her prince's devotion.

She ran to the nearest bathroom, praising the deity above it was only a single stall.

Mary was a needy beast in that moment, only aware of the pulsing between her legs. The memory of her prince on his knees flooded her mind.

How would his hair feel in her hands?

How skilled was his tongue?

What would his eyes look like as he worshiped her?

She shoved her hands into damp panties, rubbing furiously until she reached a short but intense orgasm. Mary waited until her skin cooled and breaths slowed before washing her hands and collecting her thoughts.

She was a plain girl, unlikely to catch the eye of a man, let alone his submission. That sort of thing was only for tall, attractive, slender charismatic women in leather outfits. She returned to her seat, mind and body calm once again. She didn't miss the smirk of the prince's face as she packed up her belongings.

Mary had a feeling it had nothing to do with the book he was reading.

CHAPTER 4

AN INVITATION

Mary continued her perverted surveillance until one afternoon, when a disaster of unconscionable proportions occurred.

Her usual seat, and all other available options were taken. Except, of course, for the one next to the princely stranger.

She quickly hid behind a bookshelf and pondered her next move.

Maybe she should cut her losses and move to another continent?

Certainly that would be more feasible than sitting next to her prince.

Without looking up from his book, he pulled out the chair next to him.

"You can sit next to me, I won't bite." His voice was a gentle tenor. Her loins clenched in response, but her legs remained frozen.

She had two viable choices at that moment: stay where she was now, or go and sit next to the man that had infiltrated her mind consistently since she'd first laid eyes on him. It seemed too self-indulgent, too easy to just sit next to the star of her fantasies. Surely, there was a more logical reason to talk to him.

Perhaps this was a sign from the universe that she could help him in some way?

It could be a subtle cry for help.

Mary's chest hummed at the possibility of aiding this man in any way, thawing her immobile feet.

She cleared her throat and abandoned her hiding place, riding the high of adrenaline to the plastic seat. Mary was not prepared for her prince to see her. She was suddenly very aware of the tightness of her pants, her posture, and her breath.

Did she smell? She figured she could go another day between showers but maybe not.

"Thank you," she said politely, and pulled out her notebook as normal.

Mary was conscious of his eyes on her as she uncapped her pen. Was he looking at her out of curiosity or contempt?

Was he uncomfortable with her presence?

She had never seen him talk to anyone at this table before.

Should she excuse herself and give him some space?

She took in a deep breath to steady herself and was simultaneously overwhelmed by the scent of men's deodorant and laundry detergent.

Mary's heartbeat quieted at the light and simple smell, grounding her racing thoughts.

He was just a man that was reading his book at the library and likely suffered from insomnia or a wasting disease.

Maybe he just needed a friend.

Mary couldn't do much, but she could be a good friend.

"How did you know I needed to sit?" she asked. His eyes shifted up to hers and widened a fraction, as if he did not expect there to be more conversation.

"Uh, my carbon monoxide detector went off." Embarrassment flashed through hot and heavy in her chest and under the skin of her cheeks, triggering a sudden need to strip that shirt off and burn it.

"I-"

"I'm joking," he interrupted, a small smile dancing on his lips. "I saw that your usual seat was taken."

She was shocked that he noticed where she usually sat, Mary wasn't used to being noticed. In fact, she usually preferred to be the one noticing others.

A long stretch of silence sat between them.

Though they did not speak, the hum of background whispers was soothing. She observed him out of the corner of her eye, careful not to make her ogling too noticeable.

From this distance Mary could see that the dark hair that flopped in front of his eyes was streaked with silver.

It appeared her prince was older than she had originally thought. She was still assessing him for crows feet when he spoke again.

"I like your shirt." He glanced down to the toxic green cloud graphic again, though his eyes were more relaxed this time, as if he had permission to speak.

"Thank you. I, too, like to wear the same clothes repeatedly," Mary replied, and immediately regretted it. "I mean, I'm sure you have multiple shirts that you alternate and not just wear the same dirty one everyday, because that would make you smell and you do not smell," she said with the speed, intensity, and finesse of a fatal motor vehicle accident.

She kicked herself internally—that was a creepy thing to say. He was going to call the police and she was going to spend the rest of her life whittling a ball point pen into a shiv and playing the harmonica.

CHAPTER 4

Thoroughly embarrassed, Mary stood up. "Right then, I'm just gonna go-"

The prince grabbed her arm, halting the escape attempt. His fingers were cool and slightly damp, so slender and long that they wrapped fully around her forearm.

Mary was impressed, her hands couldn't even wrap around her wrist. Though, she wasn't sure if that would be due to having large forearm circumference or abnormally small hands. His hands were definitely much larger than hers.

Intrusive thoughts of testing the size of his palm on her breast hardened her nipples.

"No," he insisted, his eyes wide with panic. "Stay?"

At that moment he wanted her to stay next to him, and she had the power to walk out the door.

Would he be disappointed?

Would he continue to think about her after she left?

Would he be happy if she stayed?

Would he smile again?

Mary had an undeniable need to make him smile again.

"Okay," she said, smiling softly. Her words must have snapped him out of some stupor, because he immediately released her arm.

He turned back to his book and she finally let out a breath she didn't know she was holding. The mysterious man had proven that he needed her company, that she could help him.

She focused herself back to her story, thinking about those long fingers, and the desperate way he wanted her to stay.

CHAPTER 4

The Prince's hands were wrapped around his Mistress' breasts, length grinding into her backside. She gripped the shelf in front of her, the pantry's musk clinging to her throat.

"Please let me have you," he moaned in her ear. "You have tortured me long enough." The wet flesh of his tongue ran up the side of her neck, filling Mistress with physical pleasure from his touch and sensual power from his blatant need.

But the Prince had not yet earned her attention, had not yet proven himself worthy.

"I have done no such thing," she replied, reaching backwards and squeezing his rigid member. He let out a tortured groan, a beautiful and satisfying sound.

"Take out your need on one of your

other women.'' Mistress would not be a play thing for the pompous Prince.

He grunted and flipped her around, leaning forward to press their fore- heads together. A soft palm cra- dled hers, pressing it to the Prince's heaving chest.

"There is no other woman in here," he said, pressing their joined hands to a racing heart. His words made the Mistress' chest throb painfully, wishing so intensely that they rang true.

The feeling was uncomfortable with its vulnerability, and thus could not continue. She was stronger than the softness he elicited.

She had to be.

"Prove it," she challenged, turning around and exiting the small pan-

try.

Mary smiled at the boldness of her Mistress. She had never been confident enough to assert herself to anyone, let alone a man. Mary truly was non-contrary.

Would she want to assert herself against a man?

Would she enjoy feeling powerful and important?

Mary rolled her eyes at her own musings. Of course, everyone would want to feel powerful and important.

"You can sit here again next time," a gentle voice offered. She glanced up to her table mate, watching him as he packed up his belongings. "If you want,"

Mary didn't let herself relish in the idea of what depraved things her animal brain wanted, but her ethical human brain definitely wanted to help the quiet man.

She just had to figure out how.

CHAPTER 5

A GIFT

As usual, Mistress stepped into her bed chamber after supper.

What was not usual was the basket sitting in the center of her bed. She peered inside tentatively, carefully inspecting the contents before extracting a modest bundle of flowers.

They were beautiful and delicate.

Her callused hands and dull nails

were a depressing juxtaposition.

She placed them in a vase on the window sill and returned to the basket, grabbing the remaining object inside—a linen wrapped brick.

Mistress carefully unwrapped the cloth revealing a fragrant bar of Royal soap. She had haggled with the merchant herself the week before, so was familiar with the rich scent and luxurious way it lathered. Despite her familiarity, she couldn't help but hold the brick to her nose and inhale deeply. The fragrance was deep and complex, and reminded her of the Prince's skin.

She hung the strip of cloth on the mirror of the vanity, a visual reminder of her luxurious man to sooth the pangs of loneliness when he was flirting with various heiresses in the name of securing political power.

Mistress longed to run her nose against the crease of his neck, to taste his pulse point again.

It would be easy for her to grab a washing bowl and run the soap over her skin, to paint an illusion of what she could be.

Is this what the Prince wanted?

To pretend that she was not one of the struts on his throne, holding him as he sat in comfort?

Did he think it would be so easy to wash away her common skin for his benefit?

Disappointment and a bolt of anger filled her chest. The Prince would not tell her what she was or needed to be, regardless of his power.

Sadness ached throughout Mary's limbs, causing a pause in her writing. She felt the Mistress' pain and doubt. She knew what it was like to feel less than, like she had to mold herself to be something to someone.

Mary refused to let her Mistress live in that way.

"Are you a writer?" a familiar male voice asked. Mary looked up from her notebook and plastered a smile on her face, shoving aside her moment of doubt. She focused on the wrinkle between his eyebrows, the expectation in those piercing eyes.

Mary's smile wavered slightly.

"Definitely not, I'm a snot wiper, mostly. From play equipment, not faces." The words came out in a clumsy rush. Mary cleared her throat, preparing to try again.

"I work at a children's outdoor playground, is what I meant."

He nodded, and returned to his book.

He looked handsome when he was serious, sharp lines becoming even sharper. Perhaps he needed her to be the fun silly friend to get him to lighten up a little.

"Are you a reader?" she asked coyly. Certainly he would understand the joke and let out a giggle. Mary would have been satisfied with a chuckle. Alas, his face remained frozen with tension.

Okay, so he didn't need a jester.

"Recreationally," he finally answered. "Professionally, I write software."

Mary nodded, both in response to him and in understanding of his character. She had befriended many shy boys in her childhood, the boring often being drawn to the plain. While they lacked social skills, usually they were nice enough (unfortunately, they also didn't bathe regularly but this man looked and smelled very clean so far).

Clearly, there was more to him that she would have to unravel.

The image of unraveling his lithe frame from a cocoon of silk sheets infiltrated her mind, causing a simmering arousal to light in her core. Mary combed her fingers through her hair, attempting to smooth away the salacious thought.

If this man was a programmer he definitely did not own silk sheets. He probably had a star wars bedspread, not sexy at all.

To her dismay, the image of him bound and gagged on-top of a graphic of R2D2 did nothing to cool the heat building within her.

Mary shook her head, resolving to distract

herself away from the unstoppable perversion he elicited.

"What else do you do, recreationally?"

"I work a lot, no time for much else." His answer was flat and dismissive, causing her heat to instantly cool with concern. It would explain how tired and hungry he looked, and Mary didn't like it.

Everyone deserved rest, even shy library acquaintances.

Lust effectively shelved, Mary's resolve turned to the real purpose of their friendship.

She nodded empathetically. "I've heard the tech sector can have brutal hours. Your job must have some PTO, at least."

The man's eyes softened at her answer, the rest of his face relaxing just a fraction. Mary's heart soared, glad that he responded well to empathy and validation, as it was something she could definitely provide him. Pleasurable satisfaction thrummed in her veins, pleased that she was able to help him, even just for a moment.

"My boss is a hard ass, but I'll see what I can do." His eyes danced and mouth pinched, like he was keeping a secret.

Mary wondered if his boss was similar to hers, with the jarring insistence of time off. Unfortunately, the dark purple that surrounded his eyes made her believe otherwise.

Maybe she could convince her new friend to go to the spa with her, he clearly needed some relaxation.

They could get those couple massages, but as friends of course.

Would they have to undress in the same room?

Mary's face heated at the image of his slender fingers undoing the buttons of his shirt.

Would he let out moans as the masseuse pressed on his tense muscles? His shoulders must be sore from all of that hunching.

Mary could also give him a massage, she was a fast learner.

The image of her prince whimpering under her touch caused a sharp prick of desire to reignite her paused arousal.

Perhaps better to let the professionals handle it, after all.

TO CLAIM A PRINCE

CHAPTER 6

AN UNEXPECTED DISCOVERY

A loud knock reverberated against the door. Mistress smirked and did not move to open it. She simply remained reclined in her bed, relishing in her power.

"You think this is funny?" the Prince spat, busting through the doorway and waving the parchment wildly in her direction. The veins of his forehead pulsated with anger, haggard breaths stretching the silk of his blazer.

He looked delicious when he was angry—a wild bull she would enjoy taming.

"I'm not certain I understand, your majesty." she lied, tilting her head coyly. He sneered and shook his head, walking back towards the door. Mistress jerked upright, suddenly faced with the potential he may walk through it, that her game had pushed him too far.

The Prince turned the lock swiftly and walked back to the foot of the bed, causing her breath to halt. His glower left Mistress wondering if perhaps it would have been better if he had left.

"No, I am the one that does not understand. I do not understand why I came to my bed chamber as usual after supper only to see every working girl in the city sitting there. Imagine my surprise to find I had apparently personally summoned them." He waved the letter around again, forehead veins continuing to pound.

Mistress rolled her eyes. "Hyperbole, there were only five."

"Five too many!" he exploded, his eyes clouded with rage as they bore into hers. As expected, the Mistress' body burned at his wildness, gaze flicking down to admire his tense frame.

"You looked wound up, I figured you could use the release."

She had to remain in control.

The Prince took a deep breath in an attempt to calm himself. He walked over to the vanity, placing the parchment on the worn wood. His eyes shifted to the opulent linen hanging from the mirror, posture softening at the recognition of its origin: the fabric that was wrapped around the soap he had attempted to gift her.

He was bewildered to find the loaf of grease sitting on his breakfast plate the next morning, unsure where he had gone wrong.

"First you return my gift, and now you give me an unwanted one," he mused, anger dissipating as he ran the satin between his fingers. "Why refuse such a generous luxury but keep the scrap that cradled it?"

Mistress crept off the bed and stepped behind her Prince, sliding the silken cloth from his hands.

He did not speak or even move as she tied the fabric around his head. In fact, The Prince's breath caught as his vision was obscured, before resuming with increased rate and depth.

"This scrap shielded the soap on its journey, protecting its delicate scent and valuable body." she murmured, stepping around his frozen frame.

Mistress didn't allow her touch to leave him, her hand trailed around the circumference of his waist as she walked. He shuddered against her palm, deprivation of sight heightening the sensation of her touch.

"Perhaps the soap would not be where he is today without the protection of the scrap. Sometimes value is not so easy to judge, wouldn't you say?" she teased, running her hands up his abdomen and around his head. She pulled gently, coaxing his face closer to hers.

"Perhaps the soap should show a

little gratitude to the scrap with his mouth." Mistress took a step backwards, the back of her thighs hitting the straight edge of the vanity. Her palm shifted from the back of his neck to one clenched fist. She tenderly unraveled his fingers before placing them on her thigh.

He followed without hesitation, letting her guide him. His touch on her leg acted as a leash, anchoring him as she perched herself on the vanity table.

Mistress lifted her dress and her thighs splayed open. "Show me your gratitude, Pet."

"Yes, Mistress," he groaned, falling to his knees for her in beautiful submission.

The Prince's skillful tongue caressed and probed at her folds, bringing overwhelming pleasure quickly. He knew every crevice of her sex, and he demonstrated it with finesse and speed as he brought her to climax.

When her shuddering ceased she removed the cloth from his face. He squinted at first, adjusting to the light shining through the window behind her.

In that moment it was easy to pretend that she was the sun that was blinding him with her brilliance, an outlandish fantasy for Mistress to entertain.

He laid his head on her lap, breaths slowly calming. Mistress played with his hair lazily, admiring the golden locks.

The false bravado had faded with her desire and now she was left with insecurity.

"It was a beautiful soap, you

shouldn't waste it on me." It was better saved for his royal skin, or the body of the wife he would inevitably be assigned. She would remain here regardless, haggling for the next batch.

"I was a fool to think I could woo you with a hunk of grease, no matter how pretty," he murmured against her skin, eyes closed in relaxation. "I should thank you for the unorthodox lesson—no one has ever challenged my mind or body in this way."

Mistress certainly hoped that was true. The thought of him begging for anyone else soured her gut.

"Although, I don't understand the role of the prostitutes in this lesson." He lifted his head from her thighs, the usual twinkle of mischief returning once again.

CHAPTER 6

A hollow laugh slipped past Mistress' lips. "Maybe I was hoping for a break from your unrelenting harassment?"

In truth, Mistress needed to test if the Prince only came to her out of sexual deviance, and to show him how she could and did coordinate the world around him. She chose not to tell him this, the test being aimed at lessening her own self-doubt and not his personal growth.

He gave her a wicked smile, shifting the longing in her heart to a deep and painful throbbing.

She loved him with such nonsensical intensity.

"Oh, I'm only getting started." His eyes blazed, lips placing open mouth kisses on her inner thigh. Heat began to stir in her core once again, and Mistress smiled, allowing her-

self to hope.

Mary closed her notebook with finality, the aching in her center too strong to bear. She caught the eyes of her table mate as she stood, and she swore his gaze lingered on her flushed cheeks for a moment before returning to his novel.

"Excuse me," she mumbled and escaped to her usual single stall hideaway. Mary shook her head as she walked, attempting to rid herself of the obvious lust-driven halluci-nation.

Jealousy twisted in her chest, envy of the Mistress and her power to play sexual games with her Prince.

Mary couldn't think of anything more desirable than their dynamic; Mistress stayed hidden during the day, attending to his needs in secret while relishing in her Prince's sensual devotion in the bedroom.

She hastily locked the door and shoved her hands into soaked panties, as she had done the previous day.

Her thoughts drifted to her muse as they always did, this time inspired by the blind-folded Prince of her story.

She imagined taking his tie and wrapping it around his tired eyes. Her fantasy self went further and shoved the currently soaked panties into his panting mouth. Mary paused her rubbing for a breath, surprised by her own depravity.

She had never considered herself a kinky person, she didn't even consider her sex drive particularly high.

Though, she could count the number of people she'd slept with on one hand, so it wasn't really surprising that she'd never orgasmed in the presence of a another before—she just couldn't open herself up to rejection when she was in her most vulnerable state.

Mary usually squeaked and squawked how her partner liked and took care of herself after. It would be different with her prince, that was something she knew with every fibre of her soul.

His vulnerable eyes would lap up her guidance, body eagerly awaiting her instruction.

The tile was cool against her back, supporting her while she gave into the fantasy. Unexpected shudders racked her body at the intrusive images of her muse flushed and needy, blinded and gagged, saliva running down his chin.

"Oh, god," Mary whimpered quietly, unable to help the words from slipped past clenched teeth. Just as she crested over the peak, a knock bounced off the door.

"Um, are you okay in there? You've been gone awhile." The worried voice of her friend was muffled behind the door.

CHAPTER 6

Mary was still convulsing when she attempted to answer.

"One-one second please,"

"Are you sure? You don't sound so good. Are you sick? I know CPR, I think."

Mary giggled, partly from his adorable concern and partly from the afterglow of her orgasm. She opened the door without further thought, still slightly dazed.

"I'm fine," she reassured him, quickly realizing her mistake.

His gaze transformed from worried to shocked as his visual inspection cascaded from flushed cheeks and damp brow down the length of her body to her clothes that were still askew.

Realization took over and his eyes lasered down to the tiled floor in front of Mary's frozen feet, a pale pink tinging his cheeks.

"Oh, I'm so sorry," he puffed out before scurrying back to his seat, chin seemingly adhered to his chest.

If Mary wasn't so horrified she would melt at his adorable awkwardness.

She was horrified, though—embarrassed and petrified, as well. She violently splashed water on her face and attempted to rub away the reality of what had just transpired.

Her prince caught her sad bathroom orgasm, and she had to somehow march back to the table as if she didn't want to crawl into a hole and die. Mary pondered the expense of funeral arrangements, death seemingly the least painful option going forward.

Fortunately, her friend appeared calm and collected when she gathered the strength to return. He greeted her with a soft smile as she sat in the chair across from him, opening her notebook as usual. Mary longed to return to the world of a Mistress who didn't doubt or embarrass herself, who was bold and smart and everything Mary wasn't.

The Prince threw a silk vest towards his Mistress as he strode into her room, not bothering to knock or ask permission. She glanced up from her knitting, posture and face a mask of indifference, though inside a tight cluster of nerves sizzled in anticipation.

The vest was beautiful, with ornate embroidering just to his Majesty's liking. It was, however, several sizes too small.

Mistress couldn't stop the corner of her mouth from pinching in victory.

"I know what you're doing," he hissed with accusation.

"You do have eyes, it is clear that I am knitting."

He ignored her comment, "You want to play games of power, show me that every part of my life is in your hands."

He gripped the fabric roughly and held it in front of him for emphasis, his tight grasp wrinkling the expensive silk.

Mistress swallowed, her mouth suddenly dry. She had been relishing in their games, enjoying how he flustered when she meddled with his meals, social engagements, and most recently clothes. Her actions were pointed and focused, pressing on the elastic borders of his control—he could easily have her executed or banished for treason, but he had simply suffered in silence.

It was intensely arousing, and gave

Mistress the rush of power she had begun to crave.

"I've had enough!" he roared, throwing down the cloth with such force her shoulders jumped. "You have been tormenting me for weeks with this nonsense." The Prince slowly placed his knees on the bed, climbing on and crawling towards her. The fury in his gaze was slowly melting to intense need.

Fear and excitement mixed in Mistress' core. Perhaps her Prince was finally at his breaking point.

"You have been torturing my mind with your games, while denying my body. I can take no more of this— you will have no playmate because I will have gone mad." He reached her feet, sitting back on his haunches. The Prince grasped one sole in his hands, caressing it gently. The fire in his gaze quieted as he pressed firm but tender fingertips to the aching arch and sensitive heel.

"I will accept your lessons with gratitude, but teach my body as well. I will be your obedient slave, but I request just a sliver of you in return." His eyes were needy, the bulge in his pants pronouncing how true his plea was.

Mistress could feel her own need pooling in her between her legs, but now was not time for her pleasure.

This was about him.

"You will come to my room every evening after supper, and our games will not leave these walls," she vowed, slowly creeping her free foot towards his straining cock. He moaned and glanced down, watching as she traced the length of him.

"But I think you can wait one more day for relief." She removed her foot.

The Prince collapsed backwards on the bed as if the light pressure of her touch was the only thing holding him up, and let out a deliciously tortured groan.

Mistress smiled and began to plan.

"Jesus Christ," a familiar male voice pulled Mary from the sensual planning of her Mistress. She glanced at her table mate with a raised eyebrow.

"I'm going to need sunglasses if you don't cut that out." His voice was stiff and movements exaggerated as he covered his eyes.

Mary glanced around the room. The lights were very much fluorescent (more likely LED, actually) and this particular area didn't have any windows, so his statement was clearly an attempt at humor.

He must have noticed her confusion because he quickly explained, "That smile was at least a thousand watts."

Mary didn't miss the pink tinge to his cheeks, and she had a feeling he knew that it was ultraviolet radiation that caused eye damage and not the rate of energy transfer.

A strange melting occurred in her chest at his playful compliment, the smile that was once meant for a scheming Mistress now pointed directly towards a shy and flustered man.

"Was that a pick up line?" Though her facial expression was deliberate (she had to make it known flirting was welcome), the mirroring blush on her cheeks was completely involuntary.

"You have a pretty smile, is what I'm trying to say." He lowered his gaze, as if the compliment had drained every drop of bravery he had.

She couldn't stand to have him doubt himself, at least when it came to her.

Doubt was reserved for serious things, like exams or if pizza was still too hot to eat (Mary could stand to have a bit more doubt about that one, considering there was still a flap of skin hanging from the roof of her mouth when she had risked a bite last night).

She reached over and grabbed his hand. "Thank you, I think you're pretty handsome too."

He let out a sharp humorless laugh.

"Okay, you don't have to go that far." He pulled his hand back, taking Mary's mood with it.

Determination quickly seeped in—it was time for her to turn up the love and support.

Purely platonic love, of course.

"I'm serious! You're a handsome young man, probably have several ladies awaiting your beck and call." She batted her eyelashes in jest, determined to make him smile again. He rolled his eyes.

"I'm thirty eight, hardly a spring chicken, and even if I did, I wouldn't know how to talk to them." Mary was surprised at both his age and his dating hesitation.

Well, she wasn't surprised that he was shy but certainly was convinced someone would have captured his fancy.

A hot bolt of jealousy ripped through her at the thought of him being intimate with anyone else. Mary dismissed the pesky emotion quickly, it was completely inappropriate for the context—he was a new friend she was attempting to uplift, the last thing he needed was her barking like a dog at nearby women.

No, this was not about Mary.

Much like Mistress, Mary had to focus on her prince's growth.

"You've been talking to me with no problems so far. Plus, talking isn't always necessary when you have pretty eyes."

"Having pretty eyes doesn't make you friends," Though his shoulders softened a fraction at the compliment, his reply was pinched between self-conscious lips. She would have to try harder.

"It worked with me,"

"That's because you're the friendliest person in the whole world, and I don't think I could stop you from talking if I tried," he teased, grabbing her hand that was still outstretched. He inspected it with his eyes and fingers, tracing the lines of her palm while his face grew somber.

Mary's mouth remained shut for once,

mostly because her brain could not handle two compliments from her prince coupled with the casual graze of his fingertips on the sensitive webbing between her thumb and fore-finger.

Could someone orgasm from touching hands?

Despite her biblical name, Mary never considered herself so easily scandalized.

"Having pretty eyes doesn't stop boys from picking on you because you have a stutter," he said, a deep grief so apparent it nearly knocked the breath from Mary's lungs.

She imagined him as a child with floppier hair and a smaller nose. Mary knew what the pain of rejection was like, knew the devastating consequences it could have on someone's self-worth.

Her prince didn't deserve to feel that way, and she had to do something about it.

"Well, I can almost guarantee you those boys are now grown men with clogged arteries and loveless marriages, and you are smart and successful and I am very pleased to call you my friend."

Mary wasn't sure when his eyes lifted to hers, but it was definitely before a look of what she could only call wonder crossed his face.

"How do you know?" he asked.

"Well, statistically eight percent of men have coronary artery disease, and I'm just making an assumption that boys who bully someone over something as insignificant as a stutter probably grow up to be insecure weak men."

"A good assumption, but not what I was talking about. I meant, how do you know that I'm smart and successful?"

"Oh," Mary hadn't really considered that her prince was anything less. "I guess because you can read."

Her full educated guess stemmed from the cumulative observations of his behaviour; he read incredibly fast, which was impressive since she spotted non-fiction memoirs and high fantasy on his roster.

But she wasn't going to say that because it was, well, creepy behaviour and she stopped wearing her "Say NO to CO shirt" for fear of smelling (the coin operated laundry machine in her building had switched to a card system which she had somehow already lost).

"You must have high standards for men," he laughed.

Mary nodded, intent on extending his happiness as much as possible.

"There will be a math test at the end of the week to validate your candidacy."

"Will I be allowed a calculator?"

"Only if you beg," The words slipped out before Mary could stop them. "I mean, if you ask nicely. And none of those graphing calculators—I cheated on a math test in highschool by using one, so I hope mental math skills aren't on your list of prerequisites for female companionship. "

To Mary's delight, he laughed again and shook his head.

"Luckily, I don't have any of those,"

Her forehead wrinkled.

"Graphing calculators?"

"Prerequisites," his gaze dropped, "Female companions, too, I guess."

Mary's lips parted at his words, genuinely surprised.

"You have no standards at all? Do you just

take your dick out at a party and wait for someone to touch it?"

He choked on a cough of discomfort and shifted in his seat. "I've never been to a party, or exposed myself in public."

That was excellent to hear, but it didn't answer the question that rattled around Mary's head.

"So, how have you gotten laid?"

His hands paused and face became bright red. She didn't know he could go that color.

"I haven't."

CHAPTER 7

MARY, THE LIAR

Mary couldn't stop thinking about their last conversation as she set up her pen and notebook the following day.

How on earth could a man at his age be a virgin?

Even ugly people had sex.

Even ugly, smelly people had sex.

She lost her own virginity in high school, but granted all she had to do was open her legs and seem agreeable.

Maybe he was born with a deformity and had no dick—it would explain why he would feel shy engaging in romantic relationships, most women needed a penis to be fulfilled sexuality.

Mary pondered if she needed it to be fulfilled. She had enjoyed penises in the past but mouths and fingers were also perfectly adequate.

"Do you have a penis?" she blurted without thinking. His bravery and openness was rubbing off on her. She started thinking about him rubbing something else off—the pale skin of his face flushed, his head thrown back in ecstasy. She imagined his whimper as he tugged on his cock.

Oh god, how she hoped he whimpered.

The room suddenly felt very warm; either she was going into early menopause or required chemical castration.

Her prince let out a strangled cough. "Last

time I checked," Wide blue eyes glanced around the mostly empty library.

Okay, so he had the tackle. Maybe the rod just couldn't perform?

Her first boyfriend had performance anxiety and couldn't maintain an erection to save his life, making the removal of her virginity impossible. He ended up having a pee fetish so Mary was grateful (not that she kink-shamed, but it just wasn't her thing).

Erectile dysfunction was also common in men as they aged. She made a mental note to search for the pathology of the disorder when she got home.

Another possible cause was religion, she knew several girls in her graduating year that saved themselves for marriage. The very devoted ones asked her to lay underneath their bed and shake it while their boyfriend inserted himself. Mary always thought it was strange that God was blind to thrust-less intercourse.

"Are you catholic?" she asked, scanning his frame for any religious memorabilia.

His eyes narrowed in suspicion. "You're trying to come up with an excuse for my chastity, aren't you?" he accused, placing his elbows on the table and leaning forward. Mary sputtered for a moment, unable to come up with a response.

No one had ever caught on to her inner ramblings before.

His bright laugh floated across the table and settled straight into Mary's chest cavity. She was quickly becoming chemically dependent on his happiness.

"Don't waste your cute little brain cells," he said, leaning back and picking up his book again. His posture was relaxed, face serene. He seemed so much more relaxed around her compared to the first day, causing satisfaction to tingle up her spine.

Mary watched him idly as she collected her haphazard thoughts that were still reeling at his confession —though it might also have to do with the way he referred to her brain cells as cute.

Mary never considered anything in her brain cute, especially not the depraved things she conjured about the man. Shaking her head, Mary attempted to regroup.

It shouldn't matter to her why he held on to his purity for this long, clearly his inexperience affected his confidence.

Mary believed that dwelling on the past was a waste of time, but changing the future was her obligation.

She was here to help him, after all.

All the pieces finally snapped together in Mary's mind. That was why she was so unusually attracted to him; the universe was telling her she needed to help him enter sexual activity.

There was no better person for the job; Mary's nonjudgmental mind and tolerant soul were perfect for the task.

She would build up his confidence with her support and launch him into the dating world dick hard and ready to experience life.

Mary chose not to think about where that would leave her.

Despite the fact that she had been watching him for nearly a week, she now saw him with fresh eyes. He continued to read, biting the tips of his fingers absentmindedly and her gaze meandered to the short stubby nails, causing her to wince (she didn't know how he could tolerate having them like that, one hangnail ruined Mary's whole week).

A vibration hammered against the table from inside her bag, indicating a call on her cellphone. Mary hurried to answer it, horrified at the ruckus she was causing.

CHAPTER 7

"Excellent news, Mary," her boss said. Mr. M didn't waste any time with his phone calls. "Your unpaid vacation is being extended another week." Blue eyes left the pages of his book and met her shocked gaze, concerned look indicating he could hear the conversation.

"What about the center?" Mary asked, dumbfounded. She couldn't imagine the man was wiping up boogers himself while she was away.

"Esmeralda's sister offered us the opportunity to start a disabled dog rehab program in Guatemala and I simply could not refuse. Surely, you understand?" he said. Mary decided she didn't like Esmeralda's sister, although she had to admire her connections.

"Of course, sir." She swallowed her rising anxiety at being jobless and turned up her empathy. "This is a great opportunity, I'm sure it'll help your healing. Good luck." They said their goodbyes and Mary tucked her cellphone back in her bag.

"Why do you look so upset? I thought vacations were a good thing," her tablemate asked.

"They are, I just don't exactly have the savings account to support two weeks of unpaid vacation."

"Why didn't you say anything to your boss, then?"

"Because he's having a tough time right now, and I can always just find some odd jobs to do for quick cash." When Mr Malinowski went on a business trip to Cancun she had spent the week scraping the dead skin off an old man's back.

Not the most dignified work, but it kept her mostly fed. The prince pressed his lips together in a deep contemplation.

"Interesting, I never pegged you for a liar,"

"A liar?" The question was almost a screech.

"You're too nice," he said with nonchalance, eyes already trained on the words of a space opera.

Mary laughed and shook her head. "There's no such thing as too nice."

The intense look he shot her devastated the confidence she had in the statement.

Was there a thing as being too nice?

How could being understanding ever be a bad thing?

"It's dishonest. Someone could disregard and hurt your feelings because you downplayed them." Pain shot through Mary's rib cage at the thought of being perceived as anything but truthful and genuine. She would rather stand on a bed of nails than hurt anyone's feelings.

"Bold of you to assume anyone has ever

cared about my feelings," she retorted, the newly formed crack in her logic armour causing a stray emotional reply to fall out.

People were usually too busy riding the high of her praise to think about her intentions.

Not her prince, apparently.

His eyes widened for a split second in surprise before dropping to fidgeting hands.

Silence stretched between them for a long moment, and she was beginning to think he was having an internal argument with himself.

"I could probably find you some work to do. It wouldn't pay much, though."

Mary smiled but shook her head.

"That's very kind of you, but I'm not very technically savvy—I would be a handicap." She would love to be able to see him more, but couldn't accept a job she was unqualified for in good faith. His laugh surprised her but the accompanying warmth to her chest was a welcome reprieve from the tension.

"Don't worry, the technical positions are filled. This would be a..." he paused for a moment to consider something. "...clerical role."

The warmth lingered in her chest. It was nice having someone try to help her for a change.

"I do know my way around an email. I can send you my resume, but be warned my Excel proficiency is an extreme exaggeration." Her googling efficiency was very high, though, so she was confident she could do the job. She reached over to her bag but his hand was suddenly on top of hers.

"Not necessary, your character reference is compelling." His hand and gaze were soft, fueling the heat in her chest.

She could get used to having a friend.

CHAPTER 8
A SHOCKING CONFESSION

Mary yawned as she sat down in the now familiar plastic chair. She had stayed up too late browsing job boards for possible quick cash jobs. Although she believed her friend when he said he would try and get her temporary income, Mary had never been able to rely on anyone and she wasn't going to start now.

Her sleep had not been peaceful, dreams filled with kind blue eyes and the background whirl of worry that she may spend the rest of her years wandering the streets and fighting with stray dogs for scraps of food.

She recognized it was a ridiculous notion (the city had a competent animal control service and she had never actually encountered a stray dog). Hopefully, the next night's dream would be more accurate—she would likely be fighting raccoons over the food grocery store dumpsters.

Mary did not do well with uncertainty, in fact she molded herself to every situation to prevent uncertainty. Even if the world was going sideways she could always count on herself to be right side up. Her friendship with the prince was quickly shifting, and she was desperate to understand what her role was (mostly as a distraction from the gnawing anxiety of living below the poverty line).

She thought back to their previous conversation, about the repeated rejections he experienced as a child.

Did he need a friend to show him that making mistakes would not hurt him? Yes, Mary was certain of that.

Did he want more than friendship? She recalled his attempt at flirting, and the few heated looks he gave her. A different conversation infiltrated her mind, replacing the lightness in her chest with sinking dread.

Did he want more only because she was a safe person?

Mary was pretty convinced he cared about her since he offered to get her a job, but did he only offer to be kind?

She was beginning to understand what her friend was saying about the dishonesty of overt kindness.

Taking a deep, steadying breath, Mary opened hernotebook, hoping that maybe her Mistress' kinky antics could distract her.

The Prince was sitting at the vanity, chiseled features reflected in the mirror.

He wore exhaustion openly, eyes fatigued and begging for comfort. Mistress' answer was to comb his hair, brushing the soft locks back and revealing high cheekbones. She repeated the action for some time, pleased that there was a noticeable release in the muscles of his shoulders. Once he was pliable, she could dig down to his depths.

"What troubles you, pet?" Her tone was light, but the eyes that met hers in the mirror were burdened.

"Politics,"

"Too complicated for a lowly common girl?" she teased, her reflection a playful pout.

When he averted his gaze, Mistress knew action must be taken.

She set down the ivory comb, pushing his hair back with her hands to inspect his face.

"What's happened?" She gripped his chin with one hand and his hair with the other. The Prince was usually full of fire, it was distressing to see him extinguished. Blessedly, he relaxed into her touch.

"I've been matched to a wife," he announced with the theater of a funeral march. Mistress' heart paused, and she was unsure if it would start again. Regretfully, the intense pain in her chest indicated it did restart.

"Oh," she breathed, still processing the implications of his words. His eyes were broken, dark with misery.

She released his head, hands sliding down and resting on his shoulders. The luxurious fabric of his blazer felt rough on her fingertips.

Not even the expensive silk she'd sourced from the east brought any comfort, the pain of their new reality too intense. She would lose her Prince.

"Congratulations, your Ma-"

"Don't," he interrupted her. Mistress was glad he did, as she was not certain she could finish the sentiment without shattering at his feet.

This was not about Mistress, however.

Her role was not to be a weak lovestruck woman, she had to serve her

Prince, even if it felt nearly impossible to do so.

"Why did you come here?"

Was this a cruel form a payback for her games?

Was she meant to comfort him with her body one last time?

"There was nowhere else for me to go." The reply was broken, almost a whisper and his eyes were pleading for salvation, for her direction.

She was strong, and right now he needed her.

Mistress swallowed her misery and said, "Nothing has to change. You will be king and no one will question a mistress."

The Prince rose to his feet in an explosion of force, forcing her to step back to avoid being hit by the stool.

"You are not a mistress, you are my Mistress!"

Mistress felt relief that the internal fire she loved was not fully quenched. She stepped forward and cradled his face in her hands.

"How long do we have?" she cooed, pressing their foreheads together.

The Prince let out a defeated sigh and squeezed his eyes closed, wrapping his arms around her.

"Early negotiations still, likely several months." A soft groan punctuated his sentence, a pleasing response to the stroke of her hand in his hair.

"Then there is no use fretting. Tomorrow may be uncertain but today, right now, I'm here and all is well," she said, planting a soft kiss on his lips. He deepened the kiss, desperate to lose himself in her.

Mistress was happy to oblige him.

"Up," she ordered, wrapping her arms around his neck. He grabbed her bottom and hoisted her into the air, walking forward and pressing her up against the wall. His tongue was aggressive and insistent in her mouth, searching for its mate and the hardness pressing into her center was begging for friction.

She wrapped her legs around his waist, grinding her aching core against his erection, giving him what he needed.

The Prince groaned into her mouth, the sound feral, wounded, and completely delicious.

Mistress took his misery into her body, his thrusts raw and savage. The pleasure was hot and the pain ran deep. She dug her fingers into the meat of his shoulder, ensuring that she was not the only one to suffer. With the breach of her intimate opening, he had released something more potent than physical desire or lustful delirium; anger began to pound underneath Mistress' sternum.

He had forced her to fall in love with him, and now he was going to leave her.

"Oh, gods," he moaned, his lips trailed down her jaw and neck, nipping their way towards her shoulder.

She gripped his hair firmly in her hand and pulled back sharply, her thoughts so wild and disjointed she could not enjoy the flush of his cheeks or pupils blown wide.

"There is no God but me." The words were intended as a reminder of her ownership, but looking into the sliver of blue that remained in his eyes, there was no doubt that her heart was under his captivity.

"Yes, Mistress," he shuttered, thrusts never faltering as he bucked into her like an unbroken horse. She rode him as such, with the satisfying knowledge that she had broken him, had claimed her Prince, and she alone had the power to put him back together.

"You are good and right and nothing can change that," she praised him through panted breaths.

He mewled nonsensically into the crook of her neck, tears landing on the skin of her collar bone.

"My Prince will remain strong, because he will break only for me." His thrusts sped up, pressure increasing to her clit. Mistress was very close, but could not go over without him.

"Break for me, pet—give me your release," she ordered, going over the crest of her orgasm in time with his. The spasms of her internal walls clutched him with a desperation that echoed in her heart, a deep fundamental need to milk every drop of his seed, to consume every part of his soul.

Slowly, they returned to the safety of the ground, though Mistress believed she may never truly return to the place she inhabited before him.

He had changed her too drastically.

Mistress would do anything for the Prince, that was the only truth she was certain about.

Mary shut the notebook, body and mind in direct conflict. The walk to the bathroom was a blur, her mind focused on piecing together the inner turbulence, rather than her feet dragging on the stained grey carpet.

Her Mistress had comforted the Prince during his time of need, just as Mary intended to do. She barely noticed the click of the door as it closed, and was unaware of her hand as it turned the lock.

Her Mistress was doing the objectively right thing, sacrificing her happiness for the sake of her great love.

Goosebumps followed the splash of cold water on the skin of her face, and the woman that resurfaced looked sad.

It was an unfamiliar feeling, for Mary to be sad for her Mistress.

Especially since selflessness was something she usually held in the highest esteem, but now all she could hear were the confronting words of her prince.

It's dishonest.

Mary dried her face with what was meant to be paper towel, but had a texture that resembled cardboard. It was rough and agitating on her cheeks, and the pain felt deserved.

You're dishonest. Her mind derived, twisting words so that the weight fell directly on her shoulders.

Mary shook her head. Putting her needs aside to help others was honorable and good.

Mary didn't know much, but she was confident in that.

She had to stay strong in that conviction or else her desire to be close with her handsome friend was entirely born from selfish lust and morbid curiosity.

Mary refused to be that kind of person, the kind that took what she wanted and lived impulsively, disregarding the pain of others.

She wanted to nurture, to make him okay so she could be okay.

Her body hummed with pleasure at the thought of being the caretaker of his heart and body. Mary resolved herself to chase the pleasure of helping him, dishonesty be damned. She would spend this week inflating his sexual ego and prove to him that letting people in would not hurt him.

That was enough for now.

She returned to the table relaxed, head and heart cleared.

"I have something to confess to you," her friend began, face concerningly serious. He looked like he was going to announce a death or debilitating disease. Mary's heart picked up pace.

Perhaps this was the reason for his abstinence—a horribly disfiguring venereal disease. She felt an avalanche of sympathy for him, assured that she could learn to love him regardless.

"I've been reading your story while you're in the bathroom."

She blinked.

That was not what Mary was expecting. Suddenly self conscious of her spelling and grammar, she thought a venereal disease might have been easier to accept.

When she continued to gape at him, he offered an explanation, "You're normally so calm, I just needed to know what could possibly get you so flustered, and well, now I just can't help myself." He blushed, gaze dropping. "I know that it's a horrible invasion of your privacy, and I am so sorry, but it is very good-" he continued to ramble, ringing his hands nervously.

It is very good. The words echoed in her mind, drowning out the rest of his rant.

He thought her story was very good.

Mary imagined her friend reading through her note book, lips parted and face flushed in arousal. Several sensations erupted in her body at the same time: her heart was pounding aggressively with the adrenaline of surprise, her core throbbed almost pain-fully with the realization that her most per-verted fantasies were no longer only hers, and her brain—well, her brain had com-pletely shut down and went somewhere far away, to someone who would know what to do and say.

Mistress would be strong in this situation, she would punish him by making him read the entire notebook aloud from start to fin-ish. His hands would be tied behind his back, forcing him to turn the pages with his mouth.

The panic receded, replaced with a focused calm.

Despite the fact that there would likely be a

puddle of arousal on the plastic chair when she stood, this was no longer about Mary.

"Did you like the way it made you feel?" she asked, interrupting him.

"Irrevocably breaking the trust of my closest friend? No, I feel like shit about it actually-" he continued to spiral.

"No, the contents of the story."

That made him pause, flush deeply and stare at his fingers while he fidgeted with them.

"Would I like a woman to be that way with me, you mean?" He didn't look at her, though it didn't seem like he was surprised at the question.

Mary hoped it was because he had thought about it before, not because he assumed she was a predator that would take him hostage and instill sexual torture on his virginal member.

Though maybe that assumption was correct, because the thought did nothing to cool the arousal between her thighs.

Mary waited with bated breath, her anticipation camouflaged under a calm facade.

Finally, he spoke."I don't want to say the wrong thing and make you think I'm a lunatic."

"Don't worry, I'm also a lunatic. I've learned that unless it's at work or a funeral it's better to just say it."

Her mind now unfrozen, it circled back to the fact that he had called her his closest friend. Friends with benefits was a thing, she was pretty sure. When her prince's eyes met hers, Mary almost died.

"I think I would like it if you did it," he said, though a loud humming filled Mary's ears so she couldn't be certain if he continued on. Her core clenched and burned. The world around her spun, and yet there was a niggling strand of disbelief poking painful holes in what should be a monumentally positive moment.

"Why?"

Plain non-contrary Mary, a sex object? It couldn't be believed.

"I'm not good at knowing what people expect from me. I guess being told exactly what to do and being praised for it sounds appealing. Simple. You're my bestfriend and I trust you, but I don't want it to be weird." He started back pedaling, doubting himself again.

He trusted her.

Honor filled Mary's chest at being given such a gift. She had no choice now but to foster and nurture that trust he gave her. She was so desperate to ease the worry of her prince, she cast her raging libido aside.

"It doesn't have to be a sex thing, if it makes

you uncomfortable. There are other ways for you to please me," she explained with a gentle smile. There was nothing gentle about the depraved things she wanted to do to him, but that was her problem to masterbate about later.

He quirked an eyebrow.

"The point is just for me to make a request, and you to accomplish it. Let's start with something small, but with consequence."

She looked around for inspiration, attempting to channel her Mistress. Her muse was picking at the spine of his book, long fingers tipped with haggard nails. The smile that slid over her face was lithe.

"I want you to paint your nails."

"I don't have nail polish."

"That's not my problem, and if your nails aren't painted by the end of the week, it will be your problem." Her voice and face remained happy and pleasant.

Would her prince really allow her to make demands?

Would he follow them?

"My problem?"

"If you're a good boy there will be a reward, if not..." He shuddered at her words, and Mary suspected it may be from the praise. This would be the first test, to see if it really was something he wanted and was ready to do.

"Would you like to be a good boy?"

He took a deep breath, closed his eyes and nodded.

"I'm sorry, I don't think I heard that."

After another shuttering breath, he finally opened his eyes.

"Y-yes, I would."

CHAPTER 8

TO CLAIM A PRINCE

CHAPTER 9
A FRUSTRATING DE-LAY

The next day, her prince's nails remained bare.

She was not surprised (she had spent the majority of the night planning all the potential choices and outcomes her friend could make).

Despite being excited to dole out punishments and rewards, Mary didn't want to rush him into making a choice.

She opened her notebook, satisfied with getting lost in the sexy antics of her Mistress.

The Prince was late.

Mistress smiled to herself, perched at the vanity once again. Her orders were very clear: he was to be in her room precisely one hour after supper. This meant the Prince was currently half an hour in arrears, causing a twisted excitement to fester in Mistress' chest and loins as she pondered the consequences of the Prince's indiscretion.

The Prince did not knock this time.

Mistress simply heard the soft open and close of the door and felt a warm set of lips pressed against the back of her neck.

"You're late," she said. She turned around in her stool, disengaging his arms from around her. She missed the contact immediately, but there were important plans ahead.

"Oh, I was just—" he began but she didn't let him finish.

She unfastened his pants and pulled out his cock. His mouth opened in surprise, heat quickly filling his eyes, and length hardening in her hands. Mistress held his handsome cock firmly, tracing the path of the veins and ridges. By the time she lavished from root to tip, he was throbbing in her grasp.

"Mistress, I-" he began. Once again he was interrupted when she slipped the tip between her lips.

"Oh, Jesus," he groaned, a dab of his essence landing on her tongue. It was sweet and salty—his pleasure was so delicious, Mistress allowed a pleased hum to vibrate around the sensitive head.

"More, please, Mistress," he pleaded, immediately realizing his mistake when she caged the pulsing shaft between her teeth and looked up at him sternly.

"If-if it pleases you." Power and pleasure radiated through her and she took him deeper to reward his amendment.

"Oh, gods, yes, thank you," he moaned, his head tilting back and eyes pressing closed.

She continued to suck and bob, his responding groans growing frantic. Just when she felt his scrotum twitch she froze and released him. The consequential groan of frustration was music to her ears.

"Mistress, I was so close."

"I know, pet." Her lips just barely grazed his tip as she spoke. To demean such an important man with an informal name was thrilling, and bolstered her sensual power.

He may be King one day, but between the walls of this bedroom, he was nothing more than her plaything.

"Delay is frustrating, isn't it?" she purred, stroking him once. Understanding flashed through his eyes, this was a punishment and not a reward.

"I'm sorry." His eyes were desperate but earnest.

"For what, my sweet?" she asked, giving the head of his cock a chaste kiss. He jumped in her hand, demanding more attention, begging for release.

"F-for being late. I-" he began to explain. She took him into the back of her throat in one deep plunge, effectively trapping him in his desire and silencing his explanation.

"I'm not interested in excuses. You may beg for my mercy," she said, popping him out of her mouth once again. Her loins smoldered with restrained lust, control wavering at the pathetic whimper her torture elliceted from between pouting lips.

"I'm so sorry, Mistress. I'm sorry for wasting your time. Please, please forgive me." His whole body shook, driven to madness by denial. She took his cock back in, bobbing slowly and evenly.

"Thank you for your kindness, Mistress. I won't disappoint you again."

He would disappoint her though, wouldn't he?

He would leave her, legally bind himself to a woman who was worthy of his love. Mistress' chest numbed at the instrusive thoughts, desire cooling.

Regardless, she continued making love to him with her mouth, now shifting her focus to bringing his climax. Her Prince deserved orgasms, and her job was to serve him as needed.

When his balls contracted this time, she let him come, swallowing down every drop he gave her.

Those few precious drops of the Prince was all Mistress would ever get. When he finished, she stood and pressed their lips together, letting him taste his release.

"You are forgiven," she murmured, wrapping her arms around his trembling frame.

Though, the only one that should be asking for forgiveness was Mistress.

'I'm sorry for falling in love with you.'

CHAPTER 10

THE FIRST TEST

On Wednesday morning, Mary caught a flash of light blue as her friend opened his book. Excitement and mild disappointment washed through her. She was worried he would make this choice.

Luckily, she came prepared.

"Well done, pet," she praised, trying out the nickname. His returning smile was heated, confirming her hunch. She inspected his hands and noted that he was meticulous, not one speck was missing or in excess.

"You've done a good job,"

"I'm going to be honest with you, I had to retry several times—it's not as easy as it looks." His smile was brimming with pride. Her heart sang, she had never seen him be proud of himself.

"You should always be honest with me," she agreed, shifting her mind back to the lesson, and away from how soft and mushy his happiness made her insides. "Do you understand why I asked you to do this?"

He shook his head.

"Do you see what a good job you did?"

He nodded, his skin pink with pleasure.

"It would be a shame to ruin such a beautiful color with your teeth."

His eyes softened in understanding, and slight confusion.

"Why does it matter if I chip them?"

"Women are very sensitive, you can't very well touch them with sharp, chipped nails." His gaze shifted between the blue nails and the inseam of Mary's pants, swallowing audibly.

"Yes, of course."

Mary's core tingled at his inspection. She steeled herself for the next step, summoning bravery—she was the Mistress, strong in her convictions and sure of herself.

"Why did you pick blue?" she asked casually, already knowing the answer. He narrowed his eyes at her slightly, as if she was an exotic creature he was trying to understand.

At that moment she felt exotic, smart and powerful.

"Because it was the least-" he didn't finish, clearly struggling with the right words.

"The least…?"

"Um, girly," he breathed out, bracing himself for the consequences of his indiscretion.

"Hmm, I feared as much." She stood up, grabbing a paper bag from her backpack and placing it in front of him on the table.

"I put a pair of my underwear in that bag." They were not especially sexy panties, plain bikini cut cotton. They were very much feminine, with pink flowers and hearts printed on them.
"You are going to wear them all day tomorrow. Work included." Mary kept her voice even as she stepped behind him, leaning forward and pressing her palms on either side of his hands, mouth just avoiding contact with the shell of his ear.

She slid the reward into his novel, a 'Don't worry be happy!' bookmark she had purchased the day before.

CHAPTER 10

"You did well, pet," she murmured, praise earning a responding shutter.
"But you can do better."

TO CLAIM A PRINCE

CHAPTER 11
GEORGE, THE
EMBARASSED PRINCE

Mary was first to the Library on Thursday morning, an unusual event.

Her mind began turning to find an explanation for the deviation, refusing to believe she had scared him off with her request.

He could be sick, everyone got the flu sometimes.

Mary had swine flu in high-school and had gone to school regardless to avoid her mother being called for an absence (she had

started a low carb diet so was a wee bit fragile at the time).

Mary remembered reassuring her mom she
was fine and not to worry, despite being
very much not fine. Mary shook her head,
disappointed in her past dishonesty.

There was an unexpected pressure in her
chest—was she unfair to her mother?

Did her mom deserve to know the truth, despite the possible consequences?

A gentle throat clearing interrupted Mary's
musings.

She looked up to see her prince, sitting in
the seat across from her. He was tense, eyes
cast downward.

Mary was so distracted she hadn't noticed
him, a first for their friendship.

She scanned the tables around them,
pleased to see that they were alone for now.

She reached forward and grasped his hand, tracing its lines and ridges with her fingertips. The contact seemed to relax him, tight shoulders dropping a few centimeters.

"How was work?" she asked, hoping he would understand what she was implying.

His eyes flickered up to her for a split second before returning to his hands.

"Hard,"

"Look at me." His eyes met hers meaningfully this time, the embarrassment plain on his face.

Mary knew this was a possibility, but didn't think it would affect him this much. She didn't think he seemed particularly misogynistic, but then again they'd only been speaking for a couple weeks.

"Were you a good boy?"

He nodded, eyes glancing away from hers

again.

"Can I see?" she asked, motioning her request to pull down the waist of his pants so she could inspect the top of his undergarments. He cleared his throat.

"I took them off, they require laundering."

Mary held back a smile, her poor embarrassed prince. She was disappointed that she didn't get to see evidence of his submission.

The image of him sitting at a computer in her panties was the star in last night's fantasy. She interlaced their fingers.

"Don't worry about it, I have plenty to spare. Do you understand why I asked you to do it?"

He nodded confidently, eyes steadfast as they held hers.

"Because I picked the most traditionally masculine color. I assumed that is what I was supposed to do, instead of asking you what you wanted," he said with surprising confidence, clearly he had been thinking about this.

Mary's eyebrows raised, she was not expecting that response.

She had assumed he picked blue due to fear of ridicule and possibly fragile masculinity.

Of course, he would act based on societal norms instead of his own wishes. Mary felt exceptionally stupid for her oversight. She did, however, still have some confusion about his embarrassment.

Why would he be so distressed if it was not due to masculinity related issues? Mary narrowed her eyes in focus.

"And what did the punishment teach you?" she enquired, aware that her intended lesson was significantly different than what he understood.

"That you're still the boss, even when we're apart." His answer was speedy, face flushing and eyes heating.

Mary's skin felt hot in response—he thought she asked him to wear her panties as a reminder that he belonged to her.

She closed her eyes and steeled herself, tamping down the deep ache in her core. This was not the time to thirst for this perfect man.

Mary vowed to add this moment to her spank bank for later.

She was Mistress right now, stoic and strong.

Mary still could not account for the embarrassment he wore so blatantly when he arrived. He clearly was not bothered by the nail polish or the punishment. Mary remembered that he was late today, which was highly unusual.

"You come here straight from work, right?"

He nodded, lips downturned and eyebrows furrowed in confusion. "Yes, why?"

Mary's smile was sly.

"So, if you had to remove any article of clothing, it would have had to be here." She rested her chin on her hands coyly, like a lion watching a mouse who would undoubtedly be a delicious lunch.

Mary could sense the growing unease in her little mouse.

"So that article of clothing would likely be in your bag, yes?" She nodded towards his laptop bag. His gaze immediately dropped to the floor, embarrassment returning. "I would like to take them, since they are mine."

He did not speak for a long moment.

"They're dirty,"

Mary rolled her eyes.

"I have a dad, it's not like I've ever seen a skid mark befor-"

"I came in them." The words rushed out of him, eyes squeezed shut. He was bracing for the expected hurt of rejection, certain that vulnerability would lead to pain.

Mary would have to change that.

She usually hoped for the best and expected the worst, but this was better than she could have ever hoped for.

"Thank you for being honest with me,"

He peeled open one eye, a precursory glance to ensure there was no emotional blow coming. When she offered him a kind smile, he relaxed.

"Can I ask why?" she asked, genuinely curious.

Many men had panty fetishes, the taboo can be quite arousing. Mary once had an ex boyfriend that would steal all his female friends lacey thongs and wear them in secret. When she found out she made him return the stolen articles and bought him his own. It made for a very interesting christmas.

He leaned forward to whisper, "Because I was sitting at my computer for eight hours thinking about your pussy."

His face had never been so close to hers. From this distance she could see the inner circle of his iris was actually a much darker shade of blue than the rest.

If Mary leaned forward even a hair she could press her lips with his.

Is that what he wanted, or was she just clouded with infatuation for him?

Mary lost her nerve and leaned back. This was about him, after all.

"I thought you didn't want this to be a sex thing."

"I never said that."

Mary paused, remembering their previous conversation. He was right, she had assumed. Mary was disappointed in herself, her mother had taught her 'when you assume you make an ass out of you and me.'

"Do you want this to be a sex thing?" she asked tentatively, trying to keep her face and tone neutral.

"I, um, well," he struggled, unable to meet her gaze. He cleared his throat and squeezed his eyes shut. "If it pleases you."

Mary had never felt such an intense wave or pleasure and happiness at his words. He was a very quick learner.

"You've definitely earned your reward, then."

She leaned forward and placed a chaste kiss on his pale cheek. His skin was warm and smooth beneath her lips. "You are a very good boy, and I am proud of you."

"Thank you," he whispered when she returned to her seat, fingers grazing where her lips had just been. He had a dazed look on his face, a light flush colored his usually deathly pale skin, and his shoulders were loose with relaxation.

He was devastatingly beautiful and wanted to be hers.

At least, in a domination and sex way. Mary's veins hummed in excitement at the added possibilities if she could involve his penis in their games.

A penis he had never used for this purpose before.

Mary had to be careful going forward, she was captaining his intimacy ship into uncharted waters. He put a lot of trust in her to unfurl his maidenhood, he deserved her full attention.

She couldn't help but imagine him laying in a bed full of rose petals, ready to be taken. The arousal she had previously tamped down reemerged, causing dampness to pool between her legs. It was now her responsibility to teach him how to enjoy his sexuality, it would only make sense for her to use herself for demonstration.

Mary's chest filled with conviction and excitement, by the time she finished with him his penis skill would cause her to scream his name!

Except she didn't know it. He wore her panties but she didn't know his first name.

"What's your name?"

"Oh, um, George."

She couldn't help but let out a laugh. His face transformed into confusion.

"I've always thought you look like a prince, it's fitting you have such a royal name. "

CHAPTER 11

"I will accept that, considering most of them were diseased and inbred," he teased and joined her laughter.

Her prince was George.

TO CLAIM A PRINCE

CHAPTER 12

THE FIRST KISS

The Prince was on his knees, which was the precise way his Mistress liked it.

The entire kingdom was beholden to his power, but she was the exception.

Mistress had never been a man's exception before, and the thought was heady.

"Do you remember the moment you became mine, your majesty?" she asked, circling around him like a vulture assessing a tasty rodent.

"I could never forget," His smile was tilted, the silk that shrouded his eyes allowing his mind to produce a vivid memory.

"Remind me, will you?" Her voice was light and casual, masking the tenderness she held for the frequently replayed moment.

"I meant to go fox hunting, but my riding crop was missing." Mistress had been in the stable that day by coincidence—the ferrier had tried to charge a supplemental fee and they had been exchanging heated words for nearly a quarter of an hour when the Prince barged in as if his bloody riding crop was a matter of national importance.

In hindsight, Mistress could have easily doomed herself to be hung that day.

"I saw you arguing with that man, and I was completely captivated."

That wasn't exactly how Mistress remembered it.

The Prince had immediately demanded his special riding crop be found, and did not accept any of the equally luxurious alternatives the ferrier offered.

Mistress stayed quiet, admiring the way his smooth skin bunched between his eyebrows as he impatiently waited for the man—who was only contractually bound to attend to the feet of horses—to rummage around the stable and produce the missing item.

Mistress knew where it was, because it remained in its usual location. The problem was that the Prince's usual groomsman had been forced to take care of his ailing wife and nobody had brought the riding crop to him in the usual fashion.

"The flush of anger stained the soft flesh below your throat, and yet you sat like a goddess at the altar, quiet with clairvoyant power."

In reality she had sat on a hay bale, waiting for either the ferrier to find the riding tool or for the Prince to call off the search. Neither happened—the ferrier continued to scurry around the stable, lifting every saddle from its hook, and the Prince continued barking out vague threats.

Impatience built in her chest, until she could take it no longer.

"And then you rose, with a calm feminine grace and produced my lost crop. I could barely even see the em-

bellished handle under your scath-
ing glare. My cock had never stood
straighter. "

That part was quite accurate.

Mistress could barely contain her
disgust at the Prince's behaviour,
and she took note of how his look of
arrogant displeasure morphed into
surprise and fear.

He hadn't been expecting her to
trudge up and hold out the crop in
front of his face as if it were a blade
and she meant to assassinate him
with it.

That was precisely what she was
thinking at the time, how tactless
and stupid his behaviour was. How
she worked herself to near breaking
point for his benefit, and he looked
at her no different than the piles of
manure in the stable.

He had no clue of her power, of how easily she could make the world around him crumble. Mistress didn't know what compelled her to put her life in such risk, but the delicious look of fear in his eyes likely had something to do with it.

"And then you snapped it, broke it in half like it meant nothing, like I meant nothing." His voice wavered, no doubt feeling both the blunt end of the riding crop she pressed between his shoulder blades, and the echo of his remembered humiliation.

"And what did I say to you?" She trailed the tip of the crop down the center of his back, relishing in the ripple of muscle it elicited.

The Prince's reply was strained. "A competent rider needs no crop, and it's only because horses can't speak that the world is ignorant to my incompetence.''

"And then what did I do?''

"You pulled me by the front of my shirt and gave me the hottest kiss of my life.''

Mistress stepped back, depriving the Prince of her touch as she circled around him again.

"It's a nice story, isn't it?'' she asked. Her voice was gentle, meant as a distraction so that when the firm length of the crop hit the meat of his shoulders, he would not expect it.

The Prince shuttered when cured leather met his flesh and groaned out a feeble, "Yes, Mistress.''

Warmth bloomed in her chest and loins.

"What was your favourite part?''

"When you ignored me for a week afterwards, despite many summons."

"Do you enjoy being denied?" She trailed the crop around his abdomen as she circled to his front, luxuriating in his panting breaths.

"No, Mistress." The crop descended from his taut stomach to the bulge in his trousers.

"Then why did you enjoy my rejection?"

His breaths were merely gasps as she ran the blunt end up and down his clothed length.

"Because I was not a prince to you, I was merely an arrogant man."

"Was this a new experience for you?"

"I have not felt truly human since I was born, simply property of the *kingdom."*

Mary put the pen down, an uncomfortable ache in her chest superseding the gentle burn between her legs. She didn't expect her simple sexual fantasy to get so deep. She shouldn't really be surprised, though.

The Prince couldn't stay a sexual object forever—he was a person, after all.

The same could be said for her prince.

She was so absorbed with the pain and pleasure of her Mistress she almost dismissed the burning of George's eyes on her. They flicked back down to his book as soon as she met them, pretending as if he didn't get caught looking. Mary rolled her eyes and pushed the notebook towards him, now that she knew he was interested.

George put his novel down and grabbed her notebook, shooting a small smile of gratitude across the table.

He was so pretty when he smiled.

Mary watched him read for several minutes, swallow, close his eyes and push the notebook away.

"I can't read this in front of you," he said. Mary frowned.

Should she excuse herself to the bathroom and give him some privacy?

George cleared his throat and motioned towards his crotch.

"Oh," Mary's mouth formed a small o in understanding.

George had an erection from reading her story.

Mary's face and center heated simultaneously, and she couldn't help but lean forward and try to sneak a peek at it.

"Hey," he snapped and covered his lap with

his book."Don't look at it."

"Why not? It is rare and untouched—likely unseen—maybe I want to study it for the sake of scientific discovery?" she joked, pretending to look through invisible binoculars.

He didn't laugh at her light-hearted attempts, in fact his eyes were sad and he began to wring his hands.

Mary had come to discover that George did that only when he was anxious or guilty.

"And what if it's disappointing?"

"It's a dick, George. They are all more or less the same."

Unless his soldier had a crazy curve to it, which would definitely be interesting.

"What if the rest of me is disappointing too, and I can't satisfy you sexually at all?" he asked, shifting his gaze to the floor. A pang of hurt sliced into her gut at his change in mood. She didn't like his self-doubt.

"Considering we are sitting in a public library I wasn't expecting you to." She tried easing his concerns with humor, simultaneously seeking to understand why he would suddenly be so concerned about satisfying her, unless it was tied to him getting an erection.

"Why, is it small?" She leaned forward, trying to steal a glance at his groin again.

Mary never considered that his equipment was simply too small to be functional.

He cleared his throat again, visibly nervous. "Perfectly average, thank you." He took a deep breath. "I guess my concern is that I don't want to make a mistake and disappoint you."

He fiddled with the spine of the book as he talked, careful not to chip his polished nails on the binding.

Regardless of the reasons, at that moment he needed her reassurance, and Mary was bound to serve her prince.

She giggled and covered her hands with his.

"You seem awfully concerned with something that hasn't happened yet."

George paused and finally lifted his gaze—it was soft and warm, much like his hands underneath hers.

"The only way you could disappoint me is by not being true to yourself and what you want. Plus, the science shows that making mistakes makes someone more likable." she spouted, unable to restrain herself. His face transformed in that moment, determination taking over.

"Right," he said.

Mary had been expecting him to pick up her notebook again and continue reading with her reassurance soothing the worry in his heart.

George didn't do that.

He took a deep breath, pulled his hands out from underneath hers, grabbed her shoulders, and pressed their mouths together.

It was sloppy, inexperienced, and frankly not very good.

It was perfect.

They pulled apart when breath ran out.

"Right," she repeated, dizziness rendering her voice nothing more than a dazed puff of breath.

"Thank you," he nodded, placing his book in the leather bag.

"You are so welcome," she replied when the lightheadedness had passed, but he was already gone.

CHAPTER 13

MARY, THE MISTRESS

Mary was experiencing a crisis of epic proportions.

She liked George, like, a lot.

Mary liked George more than she'd ever liked anyone in the past. Now that he had kissed her, she gave herself permission to initiate the next step.

She spent the entire weekend trying to figure out how she could ask him out, and continued to rehearse on the commute to the library on Monday.

"Hey, friend. I liked kissing you, and talking to you. Can we do both of those in a different location?" she whispered to herself as she walked from the bus stop.

She shook her head and tried again.

"Good afternoon, I know that I've already made you wear my panties as a friend but perhaps you could wear my panties as a boyfriend."

No, this was not about the panties. Maybe she should leave the word friend out of it entirely.

She was just pondering the sexiness of the word comrade when she ran face-first into the double glass doors that were usually automatic.

Rubbing the sore spot on her forehead that would undoubtedly become an embarrassing bruise, Mary spotted a piece of paper stuck to the glass with clear tape.

Closed for yearly maintenance

Her stomach sank.

She would have to wait for another day to embarrass herself.

Maybe they were installing carbon monoxide detectors?

"Oh, my god. Are you okay?" George asked, materializing beside her, chest heaving with laboured breaths. He must have seen her display of incompetence, and ran over to help.

Wonderful.

She definitely couldn't ask him out now.

"Yeah, my forehead's a little sore but most of the damage was done to my pride."

"Are you sure? I heard the impact from down the street."

On second thought, Mary could just walk straight into traffic.

Just when she was about to turn around and do just that, she felt arms encircling her from behind.

"If this is what you think CPR is, I think you need a refresher," she teased, covering his hands with hers, basking in the feel of his touch.

"Girls like hugs, don't they?" he said against her cheek. Mary's chest burned and her skin tingled at every point of contact with his.

"Yes, they do." This girl certainly liked them. "Looks like the library is closed." Mary said, desperate to change the subject before she divulged just how much she liked his hug, how much she liked him in general. She turned her head to look into his eyes but they were squinting, trying to read the sign.

"It appears so," he said, straightening out and withdrawing his warm arms from her torso. Her heart cried at the loss but recovered when he interlaced their hands together.

"You're holding my hand," she gaped, her mind screeching to a halt.

George didn't acknowledge her, still studying the sign and attempting to peer through the glass.

This must be a hallucination. She probably got hit by a car on the walk here, and this was the side effect of her brain's sudden and tragic demise.

"Of course," he finally said. "I live across the street, if you'd like to come over." He took several steps down the sidewalk, turning his head to shoot her the kindest, warmest smile of invitation she had ever seen.

"Okay," Mary replied, though she wasn't entirely sure she meant for her lips to move at all.

He began walking, using their clasped hands as a leash, leading a brainless, dazed, Mary precisely eighty four steps to his apartment, up the elevator and through the door.

It wasn't until she had a cup of water in her hands and was sitting on his couch that she regained the function of her frontal lobe.

"Wait, why do you go to the library to read if you live across the street?"

He was sitting a respectful distance away, his legs crossed and arms open on the back of the couch. At some point during their journey he had released several more buttons from his shirt and mussed up his hair.

Reality smacked her in the face, much like two deactivated glass doors.

She was in his apartment.

Alone.

He could murder her and no one would

know her last location.

He would be a patient serial killer, that's for sure.

George didn't really seem like the cannibal type, but she'd have to inspect his freezer to make sure. Most serial killers had mommy issues, and she regretted not asking about his relationship with his mother.

"If I tell you the truth, will it freak you out?"

Oh, there was definitely going to be a body in his freezer.

Mary shook her head—this was George. If he ate every acquaintance he likely wouldn't be so frail.

"It depends, but please tell me anyway."

"I only started going a couple weeks ago because my wifi router met an untimely death. And then..." he pinched his eyes shut and swallowed painfully. "And then I saw you behind the booth and I kept coming back to see if you were there again."

Time stopped, and all of the oxygen left Mary's lungs.

George had been coming to the library to see her.

The information sat just beyond her cochlea, yet refused to truly penetrate into belief and understanding.

There was just no way her prince was equally fascinated with her, it didn't fit into the dynamic of their relationship.

Mary's mind spun, trying desperately to rationalize.Her role was to serve him, to aid his growth. This entire friendship was about him, not her.

It couldn't be about her.

He waited patiently for her reply, looking out the large windows of his living room.

The apartment was neat and simple, like him. There were no overwhelming smells or colors and Mary felt comfortable there, like it was where she belonged. It probably had something to do with the fact that George turned his head and gazed at her with adoration.

"I see," she nodded, lowering her gaze to the cup in her lap. If he kept looking at her like that she may pass out and she really was not in the mood to test out if he did, in fact, know CPR.

He sighed and stood up, grabbing the cup from her hands and placing it on the coffee table. Mary watched, nearly drooling as he kneeled in front her, their faces on equal level, he gazed at her in an attempt to read her mind.

Oh, Jesus, he was looking at her and kneeling between her legs.

She slowly visualized every Catholic pope in descending order, a pathetic attempt to pre-

vent her from doing something embarass-
ing and horny. Just when she reached Pius
XI he spoke again.

"I've been thinking about what you said,
about doing what I want. You're right, I hav-
en't been true to myself."

Who could make such a thoughtful man feel
so unsure of himself?

Unless of course he did turn out to be a serial killer.

"So, I'm going to try to tell you what I want
now, okay?" His eyes were so blue and deep,
they completely transfixed her. "I want to
spend time with you, as my friend. "

Mary smiled, though her heart sank slightly
at his words.

She did want to be his friend, but her wan-
ton thoughts would be a challenge to control. She was making a plan to look up chastity belts online when he continued to speak.

"I want more than that too," he said, a hopeful look in his eyes. "I should have asked before I kissed you, I'm sorry. You just make me feel so bold and I want to kiss you and touch you and please you." He placed his hands on her knees, gently massaging them. She felt heat pooling between her legs at both his words and the physical contact.

She was still in disbelief that a whole human being would want to be devoted to her pleasure, plain non-contrary Mary.

"But why? You barely know me."

"I know your name is Mary, I know you take the bus everyday even though there's a driver's license in your wallet," he began. When she raised her eyebrows he quickly added, "It fell out of your bag last week."

His words turned the light tingles of his touch on her knees into something darker and hotter. Her prince was observant and she wanted him badly.

"I also know that you're kind, and patient. When Mrs. Lee comes to drop off her books you help her put them in the bin and offer to grab her new ones from the holds section." he continued, looking down once again. Despite the whirlwind of shock, awe, and panic that he had elicited, she missed his eyes.

"I know you're the most beautiful woman I've ever seen. I know that I like the way you smell, and I like how you say everything that's on your mind exactly when it gets there. I know that I've been thinking about our kiss nonstop, and more." His breath quivered but his words flowed in a righteous push. "Like how I wish I made you look like that when you opened the bathroom door."

Mary was transported back to the moment she opened that door, the flush of her orgasm still on her skin.

Understanding seeped in and Mary finally understood why he brought her here.

CHAPTER 13

He wanted to be able to please a woman, to have the skill to bring her to orgasm and the confidence to do so.

She grabbed his chin and tilted his face up to look at her. Her prince, her George, wanted her help.

Most importantly, he needed it.

The air in the room became incredibly hot and thick with Mary's anticipation. She was going to teach George how to please her, and that success would boost his confidence to pursue future sexual entanglements.

"I'm going to kiss you now and you're going to take my lead—what I do with my mouth you're going to copy, okay?" Her tone was steady despite the firestorm of butterflies currently running rampant in her stomach. She felt his grip on her knees relax, a good sign that it eased him when she took control.

She needed to take control.

Doubt rattled the foundation of her confidence, suddenly wishing she had the natural command like her Mistress.

"Do you think you could you call me Miss when we're together like this? It might make it easier to stay focused." She could be braver if she wasn't Mary.

He nodded his head slowly, his breathing getting heavy.

"Yes, uh, Miss," he replied, heat sparking in his eyes. Her sex clenched, and her resolve hardened.

She could do this.

For George.

She slowly pressed her mouth to his, a feather light touch at first. She showed him that a kiss didn't need to be aggressive to be intense.

One peck turned into two, and she couldn't

resist the urge to suck gently on his full bottom lip.

A soft moan escaped from his mouth, and Mary didn't waste the opportunity to slip between his parted lips. Her tongue performed a sensual tease, slowly exploring the warm soft flesh inside.

His tongue was shy, carefully meeting hers and caressing it but not demanding more.

The kiss was subtle, slow, and the most erotic Mary had ever experienced. What began as a small tingle between her legs, turned into a painful hot throbbing. They parted for air, and it took several deep breaths for Mary to regain her bearings.

Staying in control of George was going to be difficult if she couldn't control herself first.

"When you need a break you can trail kisses on the neck and chest." She demonstrated, cupping the back of his head while she licked and nipped a path from his ear to a bobbing Adam's apple. His groan was quiet but tortured, and had an effect equivalent to pouring gasoline on Mary's arousal.

She pulled back, checking to ensure she wasn't pushing him too far too quickly. Looking into his eyes was a mistake, and Mary should have known better.

Dark, sensual heat was caged behind irises that usually only sported doubt and fear.

She had done that.

"Your turn," she breathed.

Though his movements were careful, there was no hesitation as he curled one hand into the hair in the nape of her neck and brought his lips just under her ear. Pleasure simmered under the skin of both her head and neck, supplemented by knowledge that he was acting under her orders.

He would not judge her, would not dismiss her, would not hurt her.

A different pleasure pounded in her womb, darker, deeper, and slowly building.

Mary was used to reactive pleasure.

When she touched herself it felt good, which would begin the steady journey towards orgasm.

George had barely touched her and yet her clit felt tight and hot from the mental foreplay of several weeks of fantasy.

The pleasurable glide of his tongue on her clavicle certainly helped, though.

Heat radiated from her neck down to her chest, causing her nipples to pebble. Mary's anxiety was ripped from her head by overwhelming lust, quickly transforming her into a selfish monster.

"You can touch my breasts as well, with your hands or mouth. The nipples are particularly sensitive, so be careful." She could no longer stay on the couch, the need to be close to him was unbearable.

Her knees drifted to the ground as she relaxed into his grip and he used the opportunity to drag his mouth down to her sternum, large hands covering each breast.

The vision of his face, one she had spent so much time admiring, nipping hungrily at her flesh was almost surreal.

She leaned back to give him better access, now that his hold had shifted from her neck to clutch the side of her ribs tightly. He placed open mouthed kisses on one breast overtop of the thin shirt, nibbling at the nipple, before switching to the either.

She was needy for him, equally as desperate to feel pleasure as he was to give it to her. When his mouth neared the divot of her belly button, panic cooled her heat and allowed a shred of sanity to return.

CHAPTER 13

"S-stop," she managed to breath out, using every drop of remaining willpower. He immediately pulled away, face flushed and pupils blown so wide there was barely any blue remaining.

She had never seen a more erotic sight.

"Did I do something wrong?" he panted, eyes wide with worry. She smiled softly and held his face in her hands.

"No, pet, you did very well. Too well—I don't want to get carried away." Though she stroked his hair in soothing glides as she spoke, Mary was anything but soothed. She needed to stop before she got caught up in the fantasy of his devotion and lost her grip on reality entirely.

He took a deep breath and nodded, getting to his feet and bringing a significant bulge into her view.

A mischievous smile crept up her face—she knew exactly how to redirect the focus of her lust.

"I see you have a situation," Mary nodded towards his erection. Somehow his face flushed even further.

"Um, yes, I'm sorry." he mumbled, eyes dropping to the floor. He gripped his cock, partially to obscure it from her hungry gaze, and partially for the satisfying pressure, she suspected.

"Never be sorry, but you better take care of it." Her tone was matter-of-fact, the mask of a calm Mistress slipping back in place. "Right here." She tapped on the couch cushion next to her, urging him to sit down.

Hesitation tensed his shoulders.

"I want to watch you stroke yourself. It would please me to see you come." she said, hoping to put his mind at ease.

Though still wary, he complied and unfasted his slacks to reveal his mysterious virginal cock.

It was average in size as he had claimed. Un-circumcised, with a large bulbous head and thick shaft.

It made Mary's mouth water. She shifted to sit on the coffee table in front of him, allow-ing for a direct view of his work.

"Touch yourself, pet, like you do when you're alone." She attempted to tamp down her arousal, to offer him the warmest smile she could muster.

She wanted to stroke it, to see him fall apart in her hands. To keep stroking it even though it would be excruciatingly sensitive. She wanted to show him all the ways plea-sure could be experienced, most of which she had never experienced either.

But this was not about Mary.

George swallowed hard and wrapped long fingers around a hard shaft. He glanced up at her and waited, and it took Mary a moment to realize he was asking for permission.

She knew in theory it was an arousing concept, to be the conductor of a man's pleasure. The imaginary musings of her Mistress and the Prince made her wet, sure.

But the reality of seeing George offer her power over his pleasure and body was beyond erotic. Mary's vision tunneled and all that existed was his need, the pleasure she must bring his body, the lesson she must teach his mind.

She belonged to him, the moment he offered his surrender.

Mary said nothing, simply nodded and watched as he slowly pumped up and down on his length. Droplets of pre-cum coated his fingers as he lingered on the head.

Mary's desire made her restless, and she had to fight every instinct to mount him and suck down every drop he could give her. Instead, she allowed herself to straddle his parted thighs, leaving enough room for his movements to be unobscured. George's eyes widened in surprise, hand pausing.

That wouldn't do.

"Keep going, and don't look away." He began stroking again, gaze cemented to hers. It was very intimate, watching him pleasure himself between their bodies.

Though it was not her hand making his cheeks flush and breaths pick up speed, it felt like it was. She shifted her eyes from his pleading blues to the pale pink ridges of his cock, attempting to refocus away from selfish lust or whatever it was that she felt for George.

It was too much, no matter what it was. She needed to remember there was supposed to be a plan.

Mary closely observed his technique and

preferences, to learn how she could be the most efficient in his pleasure.

In the past, stringing coherent thoughts in the bedroom was not difficult. In fact, she had to battle intrusive thoughts like wondering when the last time her bed partner washed his sheets (too long ago) and if she had remembered to get a refill of her birth control (she had). There would be no room for errant thoughts when she was intimate with George, that was clear.

He required her focus and vigilance, and even if he didn't require it, Mary wasn't sure she could resist watching closely as he groaned and increased the pace of his hand. The pleasure caused his eyes to fall shut and head to fall back.

That wouldn't do.

Mary gripped his hair tightly, "I said don't look away,"

He came.

Without any warning or fanfare, he simply painted his hand with hot sticky jets of release.

Mary could not hold back her hunger any longer.

She lifted his hand to her mouth, licking the remains of his semen from it. His lips parted, eyes watching her intently. The heat in his gaze was boiling despite the recent orgasm. When his hand was sufficiently clean, she rested her head on his shoulder, taking several deep breaths to calm her racing heart.

"You are going to be the death of me," he whispered.

"No," she murmured back. "My mother is a nice lady."

TO CLAIM A PRINCE

CHAPTER 14

A NEW BOSS

George asked Mary if she would like to stay for dinner, and obviously she agreed.

She wanted to make a comment about what exactly she wanted to eat (not the stir fry he was currently making), but held her tongue and watched him instead.

He was relaxed, sated—some would even say George was happy.

The pleasure that hummed in her chest at watching her success was more powerful than any orgasm she'd had before.

It wasn't until they sat down to eat that his demeanor changed.

George was quiet during dinner, and Mary got the sense he wasn't used to company.

"Have you ever had dinner with someone?" she asked, trying to distract him from any self-doubt.

"Not someone I wanted to impress, and I usually just scarf something down in front of my laptop." His gaze was trained steadily on his plate. That would explain his gaunt figure. The idea of George's basic needs remaining unmet made something uncomfortable grow in Mary's chest.

He hadn't done anything to deserve that existence.

"Well, you're a pretty good cook for someone that doesn't do it much." It wasn't an empty compliment, the noodles were soft and flavourful—it was clear they didn't come from a box.

"Thank you," George's face flushed but his mouth pinched in a shy smile regardless.

Another point for Mary.

"Why do you work so hard? I thought tech paid pretty well."

"I like being busy,"

Oh, no. This conversation was approaching small talk.

Mary was abysmally terrible at small talk.

"Oh, yeah, me too. How else do you stop the intrusive and debilitating existential dread?" Mary laughed, taking another bite. Instead of joining in, George's lips parted and his fork froze just above a slice of julienned carrot.

"I mean, how's your relationship with your

mother? I should've asked when I got here just in case you were a serial killer but then we started kissing and it slipped my mind-" Mary's eyes remained fixed on her plate as she babbled, meaning she completely missed that he left his seat.

The only thing she was cognizant of was the likelihood that she would never be invited to dinner again, and then warm lips were holding hers immobile.

It was a gentle kiss, still hesitant but mind-numbingly sweet.

"It does help with the intrusive thoughts, my mom still buys me an ugly Christmas sweater every year, and tries to convince me to move back home every six months," he said with a crooked smile, and Mary's heart could be found pooled somewhere on the white vinyl flooring of the kitchen, perhaps underneath the refrigerator she now firmly believed did not hold a body.

George returned to his seat and the conversation flowed easily, a newly discovered reciprocity giving room for their words to exchange safely.

She learned that he was an only child and that his parents both worked at a bank. He considered them good parents, though he could tell they were conflicted about giving him independence and trying to help him find a fruitful relationship.

Mary blushed at the thought of George impregnating anyone.

She had never heard George talk so much, the words coming easily and smoothly. There was a painful knot just below her sternum at the thought that he could talk perfectly fine, but chose not too.

Except for Mary—she was his exception.

In turn, she told him about her own parents who were divorced but happily so. She worked hard to keep their peace, making sure not to cause too much trouble when she was a child. She told him stories of her father working late, giving her ample opportunity to watch shows she was too young for. They laughed when she relayed how her mother didn't know how to use the barbecue so Mary became proficient by the age of eleven.

"It sounds lonely," he said, bringing a stack of dishes from the table to the sink. Mary snapped out of whatever dangerous feeling was beginning to sprout.

"What does?"

"Living that way," he clarified.

"I'm not lonely, I have friends."

"Do you?" His look wasn't skeptical, it closely resembled confusion.

A fair question considering she essentially stalked him into a friendship with her.

"I did then, at least. But then they all went

to college and got married and I..." Mary trailed off, unsure how to describe the place where she was in her life.

"Stayed behind?" he offered.

Mary's heart pounded painfully.

"Yeah, somebody has to though, don't they?"

George was quiet for some time, and Mary was forced to watch the pensive frown on his face while he systematically scrubbed each plate and utensil.

"Has anyone ever taken care of you?"

What a strange question.

"Well, my parents did. I didn't starve or anything, I even got a new iPod when I sent mine through the laundry. Twice."

George shook his head. "I mean, emotionally. Have you ever had a shoulder to cry on or someone to blame when you were having a shit day?" He loaded the sparkling clean dishes into the dishwasher before leaning against it with crossed arms. She pondered for a moment, legs still pressed up against the sink.

"I guess I just didn't need that." Mary never really thought about anyone needing to take care of her. She was a perfectly capable young woman, and helping others certainly felt much more rewarding. The image of George looking up at her with adoration as he kneeled at her feet gnawed at her, though.

Was that what being taken care of felt like? Mary certainly liked that.

She felt arms encircling her from behind, and a warm body press against her back.

"Will you give me the pleasure of taking care of you?" he purred against her neck, and suddenly Mary didn't care about anything else.

She just needed to warn him of her deficits,

first. Just to ensure he wasn't disappointed.

"I probably won't finish like this—and that's not meant as a challenge—" she said, voice breaking on a moan as one of his hands palmed her breast while the other slipped past the fabric of her waistband and dipped into her heat.

"Do you want to finish like this?" Her walls squeezed around his fingers, desperate for any relief from the unreleased tension.

"I-ah, wasn't planning on it."

"Then tell me what you want, baby."

Mary had been the receiver of a wide variety of dirty talk in her life, most of it didn't do much for her. But somehow George knew exactly what to say to make her throb in an almost painful desire.

He didn't need to make her orgasm to soothe his ego, didn't see her pleasure as an unfortunate prerequisite to repeat sexual encounters.

He wanted to be a vessel for her to get exactly what she wanted. No matter what she did or asked for, she would not be rejected.

A weight lifted off of Mary's soul, allowing her to lose herself in the sensations, in George.

"Just make sure to focus on my clit and you'll be fine," she breathed, head lolling back. He took the opportunity to lick and nibble on the skin of her neck just as she had shown him earlier, his tongue eager and wild.

"Oh, you are such a good boy," Mary moaned. He pressed two fingers into her, the slickness allowing easy entry. A shaky breath puffed on the back of her neck.

"Can I use two hands?"

"Please,"

His other hand joined the party inside her

panties, flicking her clit rhythmically.

For a virgin, he certainly had good instincts.

Though just because he was a virgin didn't mean he didn't watch porn—oh, fuck that felt good.

Mary's inner monologue was forced to a halt, the pleasure her sweet George provided was tender and steady and building quickly. Her fingers gripped the counter, trying to remain standing on legs that were suddenly weak and shaky.

"It's okay, I got you, baby."

Was it the most sexually explicit thing someone had ever said to her? No.

But Mary came regardless.

She shook as stars of pleasure exploded behind her eyes, her back arching into his hard body. George held her firmly against his chest as she rode the cascading waves of her orgasm, whispering tender words of adoration as she convulsed in his arms.

He brought her down from the high slowly, eventually slipping his hands out of her underwear and carefully straightening her clothes.

There was no doubt in Mary's mind that she could fall in love with this man.

Her post orgasm trance was broken when she caught sight of herself in the hallway mirror.

"George, what the fuck is this?" she asked, inspecting the large purple and red mark on her neck.

"Looks like a hickey to me. He glanced at it with satisfaction.

"No, this is a disaster."

His face dropped.

"You're mad. I'm sorry, I've never given one and I thought that's what couples do-"

Mary didn't hear a word he said, too busy catastrophizing.

"I work with children, I can't just go into work with an announcement on my neck that I had sex."

"Technically you didn't have sex-"

"George,"

He laughed, resting his chin on her shoulder. "You've still got another week off, so don't worry about the job stuff. I'm going to take care of you, remember?" He squeezed her waist. Mary's heart quivered weakly, exhausted from all the melting and burning.

"Did you hear back from your boss?" she asked, head a little woozy from his earlier declaration.

He nodded with a coy smile.

"Pass me your phone, let's give him a call."

She obliged and watched with a silent anticipation as he dialed the number.

To her disbelief, George's phone vibrated in his pocket. She snatched her cell phone back and hung up.

"You're the boss?" she asked, already knowing the answer.

"Sort of," he shrugged.

Relying on a man she just met for an income would be risky at best and idiotic at worst. But he did seem dependable so far, and frankly she didn't have any better prospects.

"I don't think it's ethical to sleep with your employees," she said, trying to sound apprehensive about this deal.

"Technically we haven't slept together-"

"George,"

He sighed.

"You would be the only employee so the nonexistent HR department wouldn't hear of it."

"The only employee? What exactly do you do?"

"I make and sell software for commercial chemical sensors. You know, like fire alarms or-" he began.

"Carbon monoxide detectors," she finished.

TO CLAIM A PRINCE

CHAPTER 15

MARY GETS TO WORK

George's office was an office.

It met the technical specifications for a workplace, and not much more.

The carpets were gray, the walls were gray, Mary was gray.

Well, technically Mary was navy blue, but her sweater dress felt boring compared to the cartoon T-shirts she was used to wearing.

There was a desk, a handful of gray chairs,

and two doors. No art on the walls, not one hint of observable life. One of the doors led to the bathroom, the other she assumed was his personal office.

"No wonder you work from home so much, I'm already depressed," she said, running her fingers across the dusty parchment.

The desk was piled with various papers and other stationery supplies, computer monitor obscured by file folders.

"I'm not exactly the decorating type," he mumbled, clearly embarrassed. Mary was compelled to reassure him.

"Well," she took a deep breath, "let's see what we can do, shall we?"

She spent the entire day organizing and attempting to decorate the office. George gave her a very generous budget for supplies and she made good use of it.

The good thing about gray is that it matched

everything.

By the end of the week, the desk was bare and the reception area was at least eighty percent less depressing. That left Mary with the conundrum of how else she could make herself useful.

She knocked on the door jam of his office.

"You don't have to knock," he laughed, looking up from the monitor of his laptop.

"Sorry, what do you want me to do now?" she asked.

"You also don't have to apologize." He leaned back in his chair with hands tucked behind his head, looking up in deep thought.

The fluorescent lights bounced off his cheekbones, highlighting just how much he'd changed since that embarrassing day in the library.

His cheeks were fuller and under eyes considerably less purple, likely because she joined him for dinner every night and gave him an order to sleep for a minimum of eight hours (the pictures he texted her of him going to bed and waking up as proof of his compliance were just a bonus).

"Hmm, I guess my emails could probably be organized—I should be signed in on the reception computer, if you want to take a look." Mary nodded and turned back, desperate to find a way to still be useful to him.

To say his emails needed to be organized was an understatement. He had two-thousand, four-hundred and sixty five unread emails, none of which were junk or spam.

No wonder he was so stressed and tired.

Mary took a deep breath and got to work, separating the emails to appropriate folders, flagging tech-related ones for George to review.

They had lunch in his personal office, Mary

perched on his desk.

"Open," she instructed, placing a slice of cucumber inside when he complied. She watched him chew, taking pleasure in the strain of the muscles of his jaw as he did so. He didn't need to be hand-fed, but that was why Mary enjoyed doing so.

"You need another person. There's no way anybody could manage this by themselves," she said, taking a bite of bell pepper.

He swallowed and nodded sheepishly, looking down at his hands.

"I never meant to own a business. I started off as a freelancer doing small projects but I accidentally accepted a big European contract for a more sophisticated program to monitor carbon dioxide and I guess I did a good job because suddenly I had all these inquiries for my official business contact. I guess I felt like it's what I should do, since it could potentially save so many people's lives." George admitted, eyes still cast downwards.

"Why haven't you hired any help?"

George gave her a pointed look and his mouth opened and closed.

"Right, talking required for having an employee," Mary nodded, understanding why he shouldered such an unmanageable workload.

George wanted to be helpful, even if it cost him precious body fat and likely increased his risk of cardiovascular disease long term.

He wanted to suffer for the things he cared about.

Mary slid from the desk, and reached forward, lifting his chin and forcing his eyes to meet hers.

"It's a good thing I'm here to take care of my good boy, now." She smiled softly, pressing a kiss to his forehead. George didn't smile back at her, his blue eyes drifting back to the hickeys on her neck.

Mary recognized the look of guilt in them, it was one she was very familiar with.

"George," she began, stepping back and crossing her arms. "You know I forgave you, right?" His gaze remained steadfast on her neck, teeth gnawing on his lip.

"Maybe you shouldn't have,"

He truly believed he did not deserve forgiveness.

Mary cradled his cheeks in her palms, and leaned in close to whisper, "Do you need a punishment, pet?"

George swallowed, pressed his eyes close and nodded.

"Stand up for me," she said, watching closely as he complied with weary eyes.

Mary carefully undid several buttons of his shirt, revealing a firm chest. George watched her hands as she moved, eyes melting from curious to heated when her lips touched his pale skin.

His small gasp fueled the arousal quickly growing between her legs as she sucked a methodical trail on his chest.

"I wouldn't call this a punishment," he panted, eyes darkening while she worked.

Mary laughed against the space directly below his left nipple, before giving it a teasing nibble.

By the time she was done with her mission, George was a shaking mess, and there was a noticeable bulge in dark slacks.

Finished with her work, Mary leaned back to admire it.

George's chest was decorated with a large purple M, the top extending past where he typically buttoned his shirt, so Mary could still see evidence of her mark when he was all put together again.

She smiled with satisfaction. "Now we're even."

Mary could have left it at that, but she had a feeling George needed to suffer in order to achieve absolution.

Seeing him flushed and needy in front of his computer made her remember the first punishment she had given him, and suddenly it was all she could think about.

She quickly slipped her panties off and balled them in her hand. George's eyebrows raised in surprise but his eyes remained heated.

"Open," she instructed, tapping on his bottom lip. He opened his mouth, revealing teeth that were straight and eggshell white—either he had braces or was genetically gifted.

She shoved the panties between his teeth.

"Get back to work—you can take them out when we leave."

Without another word Mary walked out of his office and returned to her desk.

By the end of day she had successfully attended to ten percent of the emails on his behalf, tailing each response with her new email signature labeling her his 'executive assistant'.

Her bare ass on the gray faux leather chair was a constant reminder that her prince was nearby, suffering.

Suffering for her.

The thought burned Mary's loins and heart simultaneously. She imagined his cock throbbing in his pants, begging for her attention.

She was just about to open another technical support ticket when two warm hands landed on her shoulders, making her swivel the chair around to face her prince.

For the first time since she'd met him, George was standing with no hunch in his back.

Mary looked up at his form, confidently guessing he stood at five feet and ten inches. Another part of him was also standing very tall, but Mary chose to ignore it for now.

Her eyes focused on his face, and she immediately regretted it.

The cloth remained wadded in his mouth, with thin rivulets of saliva having escaped over hours, leaving faint pink trails of irritation down his chin and neck. Mary's eyes followed the sensual trails, leading to a shirt so soaked with saliva it clung to his skin, turning translucent enough to reveal the bruised initial marking his chest.

Mary imagined how it must itch and burn,

the wetness being forced to pool there. That in itself was so arousing she wanted to part her already slick thighs and find release of it, but then her eyes landed on his.

The irises that were usually a calm lapis were nearly black with hunger and seemed to look past her, like she had taken him somewhere else entirely.

He was an erotic masterpiece that Mary never knew she could create.

She ignored the infernal blaze in her core, it was time to bring her prince back.

Mary stood and flattened her palm in front of him, signaling the punishment was over. The fabric dropped from his mouth and landed in her hand with a wet smack.

She carefully slipped the wet undergarments on, relishing in the depravity of his slobber on her most intimate place.

He watched her with precision, face still blank.

"Sit," Mary said, pointing at her desk chair. He plunked down with such exhaustion, it seemed more like a collapse than anything else.

Power and heat pounded through her veins in tandem as she rummaged in her bag for a packet of hypoallergenic face wipes (useful on the rare occasions she wore make-up). She carefully straddled his thighs and wiped away the evidence of his submission, both saddened that it was gone but relieved that he would be comfortable.

Once he was cleaned up, she peppered sweet kisses to his cheeks and chin, before tucking his forehead into the crook of her neck and running one hand through his hair in tender swipes.

"You are a good boy and I am so proud of you," she murmured tenderly, and continued to do so until he lifted his head and pressed a deep kiss to her lips.

"Thank you," His face was still flushed and tender, but his eyes were no longer distant, simply lethargic. "Let's go home?"

Mary was brimming with pride, pleased at her competence and ability to help her prince.

Her boyfriend.

Was he her boyfriend?

So far he was only confirmed to be her friend and submissive. Mary suddenly realized that he may not be interested in her romantically at all. They never really talked about it, just slipped into new roles that revolved around each other.

Did she want him to be her boyfriend?

It wasn't until he had pressed the button on the elevator of the apartment that she gathered the courage to ask.

CHAPTER 15

"What are we?"

"Riding in the elevator," George said. She rolled her eyes and smacked his arm.

He laughed and wrapped his arms around her waist.

"You are my salvation, and I am your helpless servant," he said, nibbling on the side of her neck. She laughed and pushed him off.

Silly George was new but she liked him.

"I'm serious, how should I introduce you to people?"

He pressed their lips together softly, lingering a moment to nibble on her lower lip. The tingle of an unreleased orgasm sprouted in response.

"However you like, sweetheart," he said between kisses. He began to trail his kisses down her neck to her cleavage. She ignored the fire burning in her sex.

"Oh, hello, this is George, my boss slash sex slave," she imitated, breathing becoming labored from his attention.

"I think we have firmly established that you are the boss," he murmured against her nipple that he was currently nibbling on. She rolled her eyes again.

Clearly, he was not capable of serious conversation when he was drunk on his desire.

His hands drifted to her ass, kneading each cheek firmly. Mary let out a small moan, gripping the back of his head.

Panic began to build in her belly at how weak he was beginning to make her—he could easily shatter her completely and she couldn't do anything to stop it.

Luckily the door to the elevator opened, saving his virginity (and her sanity) for the time being. They separated suddenly, panting. He grabbed her hand and led her to his apartment.

CHAPTER 15

"Come on, there's work to do."

George wasn't kidding about doing more work.

Not even an hour after they returned, he was sitting on the end of the couch, fingers tapping furiously across the keyboard of his laptop.

Mary let her eyes roam his figure, appreciating the strength and severity of his features. He changed into a t-shirt and sweatpants as soon as they walked through the door, muttering something about not liking dirty clothes on his couch. He never made any comment about her clothes, but she started bringing a change of clothes, anyway. The smile he gave her was worth the extra trouble.

Mary opened her notebook, prying her eyes away from her George.

"I brought you a gift." The Prince said. Mistress looked up to see an open jewelry box in his hands. "I beg you not to return this one with prostitutes."

A string of gold was resting on a pillow of velvet. The necklace was large and opulent—it did not belong on her common skin.

Mistress shook her head.

"It will be a scandal."

"So let it!" he exclaimed, clearly exasperated by her continued objections.

Oh, how she wished it didn't need to be this way. Mistress longed to accept the precious jewelry, but the consequences were simply intolerable.

"And how will I live with myself if you lose everything because of me?" she asked, losing the fight to remain strong and unaffected.

"How will I live without you? I cannot. I cannot keep living this lie that my heart and soul is still my own." The Prince's skin was flushed with desperation, a beautiful, heartbreaking sight.

He wanted a visible reminder of her possession, needed it so badly he was ready to sacrifice his place as heir to the kingdom.

Mistress had an idea, desperate to ease the heartache of her love. She took the box from his grip, removed the burden of it from his hands so she could lead him to the vanity.

The Prince sat and watched her reflection in the mirror, his pupils following closely as she removed the necklace from its container and placed it around his neck.

It glinted in the afternoon sun, the rays reflecting off both the gold metal and the golden locks of his head.

"You wanted me to wear this to show your ownership, didn't you?"

The Prince didn't answer, simply lowered his eyes to the floor.

"It was a sweet but misguided attempt, pet."

He should know there was never a world where their love could be loud and honest.

She fastened the clasp at the nape of his neck, giving the flesh there a firm squeeze. The Prince closed his eyes and his head became heavy with the pleasure of her touch.

"This is what I want you to feel when you are going about your day." Another squeeze, just above the band of gold. "The whole world will be able to see it, but only we will know its significance. You will be able to feel its weight and remember that you're mine."

She gave his neck a final squeeze and removed her grip.

When the Prince's eyes opened again, his gaze was heated and the groin of his pants firm between them.

"I'd rather wear your legs around my neck, but it'll do."

Mary felt sympathy for the Prince—she was also struggling with being only one facet of George's life—but she also felt something for his Mistress, who was grasping to find ways to remain in her Prince's life.

Mary wasn't sure who she was meant to identify with in her fantasy, just as she was unsure what her purpose was with George.

He wanted to take care of her, and Mary didn't know what to do with that.

He had managed to see into her more deeply than any other person ever had, which was just as frightening as it was thrilling.

She looked up at him, carefully studying his form in hopes that she would suddenly lose interest now that he was significantly healthier and happier.

His shoulders were raised, a curve to his upper back. Mary glanced up to the square analog clock above the TV.

He had been working for several hours, clearly he was becoming fatigued. His typing remained furious, no sign of stopping to rest.

Despite the improvements she had made to his life and routine, there was still more work to do.

Truthfully, she was also craving the escape that her written fantasy didn't provide.

Mary stood. The notebook fell to the floor, causing her prince to look down at it. His gaze then lifted slowly up her bare legs and ended at stern brown eyes.

"Pet," she said, walking over and placing gentle hands on tight, hunched shoulders.

"Miss," he replied, groaning as she pressed a thumb into each bunched trapezius.

"Do you know why I make you eat and sleep to my pleasure?"

George didn't answer, merely shook his head with closed eyes. She continued to massage, his sighs of pleasure igniting the sensual fire of power within her. She had him quivering under her frustratingly small hands, and she might as well have the entire world in her grasp.

"Because I take care of what's mine." Her voice was a subdued hiss, and she hoped he didn't remember her story of putting an iPod in the washer multiple times.

"Y-yes," he shuddered under her firm minis-trations.

Mary shifted herself and sat in the corner of the couch, parting her legs.

"Watching you suffer makes me hungry, and

I don't appreciate you wasting it on your work. Who does your suffering belong to?" Mary had intended for the words to be a theatrical exaggeration, a part of a sexual scene for his comfort and benefit. But she didn't spot even a tinge of dishonesty in her heart as she said it, she was greedy for his suffering.

She wanted to have all of him.

George's head was thrown back over the end of the chair, bringing his face in perfect and yet opposite alignment with hers. She could easily press her lips to his chin and further. The lump in the center of his throat bobbed as he swallowed and Mary felt a deep primal hunger to sink her teeth into it, rip it from his body and free his voice.

Moisture dampened her panties.

"Y-you," he said, though it was barely more than a whisper. Her hands drifted from his shoulders to the back of his neck, just as the Mistress had done with her Prince.

Though, there was no necklace of ownership collaring her prince's throat, and there never would be.

Because as much as she wished it was different, this story was not about Mary.

"I'm sorry, what was that?"

George's eyes opened and the same moment he spoke, giving her a painful jolt to the chest.

"You, everything belongs to you." Hot, greedy, pleasure licked up the column of her spine and settled in her womb with a pool of forbidden arousal.

"So, why do you think it's okay to damage what belongs to me?"

"I'm sorry-"

"I didn't ask for an apology, I need an explanation."

His eyes scanned her face for a moment, as if deciding how much information to divulge. Mary wanted everything. Her palm shifted to cradle the underside of his chin firmly.

"I didn't realize it mattered,"

"Everything you do matters to me, George." Though her voice was still dropped in a sensual hiss, the place the words escaped from had nothing to do with her inner Mistress. His eyes widened in surprise and Mary had to change the subject.

She leaned forward until her lips were hovering above his.

"How can you eat my pussy if your neck is tight and sore from overworking?" She pulled back, pleased to see that the skin of his cheeks was flushed and the rate of his breath had increased.

"I don't know, i've never-"

"Do you still have work to finish?" She cut

him off, the pounding between her legs brewing impatience.

"Just some emails,"

"Well, the sooner you finish, the sooner you can make me come."

His head snapped straight, and hands resumed their furious typing. Mary had to hold in a laugh at his eagerness.

She pressed one hand to the spot where his neck met his clavicle, the other hand planted firmly in his hair. She ran her hands softly through the silky strands idly as she watched the long digits work quickly against the keyword, and as expected, his shoulders began to bunch against her palm.

Mary bent forward to whisper in his ear, "If I feel you tense up, I will pull."

She demonstrated, tightening her hold on his head. He gasped at the new sensation, but relaxed his shoulders immediately.

"Keep working,"

They continued the erotic dance, her tuggs of reminder like a rider pulling the reins of an overzealous steed.

He needed her reminders approximately every ten emails, consequently letting out a sharp breath and a moan each time, which reverberated in her pussy.

By the third pull, the aching inside was unbearable and she could clearly see a straining erection in George's sweatpants, the thin cotton doing nothing to hide it from her hungry gaze.

Despite George being the subject of punishment, Mary was nearly shaking with the repeated sexual denial of his submission.

"I'm done," he whispered, closing the laptop and ridding his lungs of an exhausted breath.

Not a moment too soon.

Mary backed up and stood next to the couch.

"Undress me," It was a simple command, but George looked at her as if she had asked him to kiss a handful of live snakes.

He had no reason to be scared, she even shaved her pubic hair for the occasion.

"You're scared. Are you worried my body will disappoint you?" Mary hadn't been worried about it, but she struggled to explain the petrified look on his face.

Men typically didn't hesitate to get a woman naked.

He stood and walked to join her, stopping when she was within reach. George didn't extend his arms to follow her command, simply looked at the floor and bit his lip.

"I'm worried my body will disappoint you." Mary knew he wasn't concerned of her attraction to his form, he was referring to the use of his body in carrying out her commands. He had never undressed anyone, had no point of reference on how to do it right. Mary's lust had gotten the best of her, and she had forgotten the point of their entire relationship.

"Would it help if I showed you, first?"

He nodded but his eyes didn't leave the floor.

That wouldn't do.

Mary grabbed his chin, lifting it until she had him again.

"You can't learn if you don't watch." It was such a simple sentence and yet described a fundamental belief she held. It was why she watched him in the library so closely, seeking to understand him.

Or maybe, it was herself she didn't understand.

Maybe this had nothing to do with George at all.

She released her grip and his eyes followed obediently as she pulled the hem of his shirt up and above his head, before folding it and placing it on the coffee table. She repeated the steps with his sweatpants but decided to leave his boxers on for both of their benefits.

"Okay, your turn."

George nodded, and began his mission.

Mary nearly had to close her eyes—there was something so primally arousing about the image of his skin remaining taught overtop muscles shifting with the effort of removing her clothes.

He folded the shirt and shorts with precision and set them next to hers on the table, leaving her undergarments untouched—a perfect mirror of her demonstration.

Before she did something stupid, Mary

turned and reclined on the couch. When he didn't move, she decided he needed some reassurance.

"I won't let you fail. Just do what I say and I will be very, very pleased."

She could see the goose flesh that pricked his skin at her words, a pleasing contrast to the way his reservations melted and he positioned himself between her spread thighs.

"Start with chaste kisses, a woman's desire isn't often spontaneous." Her desire seemed to be perpetual, but she was training him for his real upcoming love, so that didn't matter.

The first contact did not involve his lips at all.

He ran the tip of his nose from the apex of one thigh to the other, lingering only for a moment on her panty-clad sex. Heat that was already a barely controlled simmer rose from a place deep inside to the surface of her skin, sensitizing it to his touch.

He had followed her implied command of beginning with a tease, but Mary was too worked up to commend him for it. Just when she was about to pull his hair and restate her instructions, he pressed sweet kisses in the same pattern. Her neglected pussy quivered beneath his attention, begging for more.

Mary could not beg, George needed a strong confident teacher.

"When she's adequately turned on, you can increase the pressure, even incorporate a nibble or two. Do you know the signs to look for?"

George lifted his face from her skin, a momentary reprieve from the building pleasure, only to devastate her with a dark, hungry look.

"Her breathing gets faster and she looks at me like I'm prey."

"Prey?"

George nodded and nuzzled his face against the fleshy mound that protected her sensitive clit. Mary wanted to moan and thrash, but she simply bit her lip instead. That answer was both surprisingly good and heartbreakingly bad.

Good for Mary, but unhelpful for his sexual confidence.

"There are other signs, as well. She might sigh and moan, whimper and plead." Mary's hands buried in his hair, needing to speed this lesson along before she lost her mind entirely.

"Or she just bites her lip to keep it hidden." George said against the skin above her femoral artery, making a painful pounding in her chest join the one between her legs.

That was enough.

Her grip on his hair turned cruel, "Eat my pussy, now."

He wasted no time pulling her panties to the side and diving in, his movements enthusiastic but unfocused.

"The top, suck and flick my clit with your tongue," she said, and he obeyed an unexpected finesse. He was a very fast learner, lapping quick focused circles on her most sensitive spot.

"May I use my hands?" he asked, resurfacing to take a panting breath.

"Yes,"

The smile he gave her was brilliant and wide, triumphant and free.

Mary had received oral sex before and it was usually physically pleasurable (it was hard to make a hot, wet, mouth feel bad).

But orgasms were not even in the picture then, there were too many unknowns, and she couldn't let go enough to build an orgasm while still focusing on how to appropriately portray herself.

With George, all she could do was focus on her own desire, because he needed her pleasure. There was no threat of unpredictability because he was not operating under a psyche she had to understand and anticipate—his touch was simply an extension of her own hand, the orders of non-contrary Mary who was helpful and well-behaved, who never hurt anyone under any circumstance.

He was safe and so was she.

She was also getting embarrassingly close to said previously unattainable orgasm, likely because he started rhythmically caressing her inner walls with his fingers.

He continued to worship her clit with his tongue and teeth and the sight of her prince between her thighs was more potent than she was ready for. She looked away from his tongue lapping at her, attempting to gain control.

It was then she noticed his hips gyrating.

A perfect distraction.

"You're fucking against the cushions, baby. Does eating my pussy make you hard?"

He moaned his agreement between licks.

"If you're not careful you're going to come, and that would be very disappointing."

His hips stilled.

Mary thought the distraction away from the pleasure he was bringing to her pussy would keep her climax at bay, but watching how wholly she could control him had a familiar tingle beginning in the soles of her feet.

"Don't stop," she ground out through clenched teeth.

He didn't.

George didn't change the pace of his actions

in any way, just moaned and swallowed every drop of her arousal.

The spasms of release seemed to go on forever, though likely only a minute or so.

When her breathing had sufficiently calmed, she began stroking his hair (he had shifted to rest his head on her thigh when her poor overstimulated clit could take no more).

"Do you understand now why it's important to pace yourself?" Her voice was quiet, sated and lethargic.

He hummed against the damp skin of her inner thigh. "Because my work is not limited to my laptop."

Once again, his understanding and her intention for the lesson were starkly different.

She didn't correct him, just continued to stroke his hair and let herself be comforted by the predictable sounds of his breathing.

TO CLAIM A PRINCE

CHAPTER 16
A BITTERSWEET ENDING

"Open wide, pet." Mistress instructed, placing the ball of chocolate in the Prince's mouth. He complied and moaned as he chewed. Mistress repeated her action twice more with a grape and a slice of apple.

She was sitting with her legs outstretched and parted comfortably, feeding her Prince.

"Please, no more, or you'll have to fetch the carriage just to get me down the hill," he pleaded, stretching out on the cotton blanket and resting his palm on a taut stomach.

The sun bounced off the opal buttons of his undone shirt, giving the air of luxurious lethargy. The Prince looked relaxed, inhaling the valley air with easy breaths.

He had convinced Mistress to accompany him to the fields under the pretense of assessing the possibility of planting sunflowers next season. He then led her straight past the crop fields to the patch of long grass that overlooked the river. He surprised her again by pulling out all the supplies for an impromptu picnic from his canvas bag.

It was nice.

CHAPTER 16

Sitting in the sun, enjoying the re-freshing air and each other's company, they were simply two souls.

They could have been anyone, any two lovers having a romantic date by the river.

But the Prince wasn't just anyone, and Mistress was no one at all.

"How are you feeling?" she asked, hoping to avoid more thought on her own feelings.

"A bit warm, actually. Do you have a fan hidden somewhere in your dress? I require cooling." He wiped the back of his hand on a damp forehead.

Mistress rolled her eyes, "Right away, your majesty," she said and reached over to grasp one of the water glasses.

The Prince's eyes remained closed,

giving her the element of surprise when she dumped the cool liquid on his chest.

His shriek of shock and outrage pierced her loins, a pleasing reminder of how she could affect him.

"Hey, what was that for?" He sat up abruptly. The newly wet shirt clung to his chest, rivulets of water trailing down towards the tidy trail of hair above his groin.

"Being a pest," she replied, unable to keep her eyes from his half naked and now damp form. The Prince noticed her gaze, face lighting up with mischief.

Mistress did not like this at all.

He slowly rolled to his knees, crawling in her direction. The Prince on his knees had not yet lost its appeal, an ache now pounding deep in Mistress' womb.

"An act of assault on the future King," he began, adding a haughty lilt to his voice. Mistress narrowed her eyes—a playful Prince meant trouble.

"I could try you for treason right now."

He continued crawling forward until his face was mere centimeters away.

"But you are no common criminal," Icy blue eyes raked the length of her body, an uncomfortable prickle re-placing the lingering warmth from the sun.
"I know a witch when I see one."

She was trapped both physically and mentally by him, a moon orbiting painfully around the blazing heat of her star.

His love threatened to burn them

both alive.

"Do you know what we do with witches? Drown them." He upturned the entire pitcher over her head.

"Ack!" Mistress sputtered and gasped, pushing her now soaked hair out of her eyes.

Before she could even open them, his lips were crushed to hers and she was pushed onto her back.

They were a flurry of hands and need, wet clothes being removed and landing in the tall grass with a soaking plop. Desperation clouded her judgement, leaving only enough room for needing him.

She needed him closer, to absorb him into her soul where he could remain safely tucked away.

Her mouth opened on its own accord, inviting his tongue to plunder the moist tender flesh inside.

He accepted the invitation, plunging his cock into her soaking depths in tandem with the insistent exploration of his tongue.

She clenched around him, arousal allowing him to be fully seated immediately.

They sighed in unison, the comfort of rightness and relaxation of coming home at last.

The Prince had power to rule the entire kingdom, and yet it was in her body he sought his solace.

Mistress could feel every inch of him, despite the savageness of his thrusts and the blinding pleasure they provided. She felt his soul.

Though the embrace was intimate,

this man was not making love to her—he was seeking his freedom in her body.

"Free me from this charade," he moaned into her neck.

Mistress wrapped her legs around his waist, urging his thrusts deeper and cradling his suffering in soft, strong thighs.

Her duty was to serve him, but her compulsion above all else was to love him.

"Please, witch, take me away—wave your wand and turn me to a toad so I may travel in your pocket."

His thrusts grew frantic, hitting Mistress in a place inside so deep it brought tears to her honey brown eyes. As if sensing her fracture, the Prince lifted his head from the sensitive place under her ear and kissed the wet trails she did not mean to let escape.

"But please don't kiss me, please keep me forever," he finished with a broken sigh, forehead pressed against Mistress.'

She wanted to scream that she could never live without him, that he would always have a place in her heart, that her last breath would be reserved for whispering his name.

But she couldn't.

Because despite the shout of his release as he gave her his seed, he didn't really belong to her. Despite his sweet words and complete devotion the Prince was never meant to be hers.

Despite their dance of power and submission, the Prince would never be hers to claim.

Mary looked up from the notebook, tears prickling in her eyes.

She knew that it was time to detach from George's life, that she had taught him all that she could.

Well, almost.

They still hadn't had sex.

Life with George had fallen into a routine.

She would attend to his emails at work, he would attend to her pussy from underneath the reception desk.

They would come back to his apartment where he had an orgasm ripped from him in one perverted challenge or another, followed by dinner and one more mutually shared climax.

Mary was delaying his deflowering, still unsure on how to make it perfect enough, and fearful of what came next. If she were to complete this final act, there would be nothing he would really need her for.

Mary knew a lot of things, but how to keep someone's attention wasn't one of them.

She was accustomed to "Thank you for all the help but I'd like to get a blowjob from my neighbor now."

Okay, so that only happened once but surely this dynamic couldn't go on forever. It was only a matter of time before he moved on to greener, smarter, more enticing pastures.

Pastures that didn't work minimum wage jobs, that were able to give him everything he deserved.

Mary was the calm and George was ready for the storm.

After they took this next step there would be nothing left to teach, nothing for Mary to justify her position in his life.

"It's getting late," he called out from the kitchen. Mary wiped her face roughly and stood, walking over to put an arm into her coat.

"Would you like to stay the night?" he added, unexpectedly.

She didn't answer, taking a moment to process the request.

He wanted her to stay over.

She would be sleeping in his bed.

Next to him.

He wanted to sleep with her.

"Baby?" He poked his head out into the hallway. His cheeks were fuller than she had ever seen, and the purple under his eyes was just a pastel shadow.

Those eyes were bright, if not a bit con-cerned at the moment.

He was so perfect.

Satisfaction dulled the heartbreak, giving her a small moment of solace in what would undoubtedly be her darkest night.

She did that.

"Do I want to stay the night?" she repeated, fastening the zipper of her jacket.

"Yeah, you know, you sleep in my bed in-stead of yours."

Mary's heart thudded painfully in her chest.

"Why would I do that?"

"Because that's usually how sex happens." He walked over and pulled her into his arms.

A hit of adrenaline coursed through her.

She wanted to deflower him, but the thought of doing it now felt akin to putting her own head into a guillotine.

"You're not ready," she said, eyes dropping to avoid seeing his reaction.

"Pretty sure I am," He grabbed her palm and placed it on a cotton covered erection.

Mary swallowed, desperately trying to think of a way to delay the end of their arrangement.

"George, I really don't think we should rush this. I promised myself when we met that I would take care of your inexperience with patience." Her words came out rushed, as they usually did when she began to panic.

"What does that mean?"

"Well, you seemed so lonely and I knew you probably wouldn't get another chance."

"Whoa, hold on." He gripped her by the upper arms.

"You started fooling around with me just because I was a sad, lonely, virgin?" His voice was high pitched and incredulous.

"Well, sort of, yes." Mary avoided his angry gaze.

"I've been a pity fuck this whole time?" he spat, letting go of her and pressing his palms over his eyes in exacerbation.

"Well, technically we haven't fu-"

"Mary," he interrupted, eyes as cold and blue as ice. "Do you even want me?" George's voice was quiet, the pain evident in his tone.

She cleared her throat and clutched her bag tight to her breaking heart.

"You needed me, that's more important." She had repeated that phrase to herself so many times it became a psychotic mantra.

"No, I didn't." He turned away and walked towards the living room.

Mary stepped towards the door, leaving her shattered heart on the carpet of his hallway.

"Right, sorry for the misunderstanding."

CHAPTER 17

A DARK NIGHT

Mary crossed the street outside George's apartment, landing her in front of the library.

She wouldn't cry.

Her Mistress would never cry about the logical end to a whirlwind love affair.

She was so numb from shock and heartbreak that she barely noticed her phone ringing as she passed by the main doors.

Mary sighed, pulling out her phone and sitting on the curb.

"Excellent news, Mary." Mr. M's exuberant voice was shrill in her ear. Mary felt like there may never be true excellent news ever again.

Unless he was going to announce that a hit-man was stationed on the library roof and was about to blow her brains out.

"We are on our flight home, and I expect to see you back on that foam mat bright and early tomorrow morning," he continued, with the same forceful excitement she expected.

"Okay," she mumbled and ended the call, unable to pretend at that moment.

Mary was so tired of pretending.

Pretending to like her job, and her shitty apartment.

Pretending she wasn't hopelessly and completely in love with George.

Pretending that she didn't just ruin her chance with the only man who saw her, understood her.

She threw all of it away, and for what?

To be a good, helpful person?

No, Mary decided she wasn't a good person—she was a coward.

Her Mistress was a coward too, choosing to give up the Prince she loved just because their love wasn't simple.

The urge to cry returned, and this time there was nothing to stop her from giving in.

She dropped her head into her hands and wept, grieving the short preview of a life she almost had. She knew that she should get up and go to the bus stop, return to the life she was supposed to be living.

But Mary didn't want to.

She didn't want to go back to her shitty apartment, her shitty job, or her nonexistent social life.

She didn't want to be that dishonest girl who said she was happy with nothing.

She wanted to be the new woman that George had created, who was honest and direct with her feelings, who always knew she would be seen and understood.

She just wanted George, and everything that came with him.

Mary pulled out her phone again, knowing exactly what needed to be done.

"Excellent news," she said, tone flat. "I quit." Righteous energy flooded her limbs and she threw the device at full velocity into the concrete outer wall of the library.

CHAPTER 17

It smashed into hundreds of plastic shards, satisfying some primal urge to destroy.

Now her phone felt the same way her heart did.

Even if George never forgave her, at least she could start working towards being the woman he falsely believed she was.

Mary could do this.

For herself.

TO CLAIM A PRINCE

CHAPTER 18

A NEW BEGINNING

"George!" Mary screamed, thumping her fists against the wood surface of his door. She didn't care how long it took, she would get him to talk to her.

"I want you," she cried, pounding loudly. "I've wanted you the whole time, since I slipped on those stupid pamphlets."

The door opened.

"Was that so hard?" George asked, voice soft and no longer angry.

"Incredibly," Mary answered, throwing herself into his arms. He caught her and stepped backwards, taking them inside.

"I'm so sorry, George," she sobbed. "I just didn't want to hurt you–"

"No, you didn't want to get hurt," he amended, setting her back down on the floor. Mary nodded, acknowledging that he saw through her in that regard too. "Letting someone in is difficult, if anyone knows that it's me."

"George, I'm-" He silenced her with his lips this time, willing her to relax in his arms.

"You misunderstood my words," he said when they parted for air.

Though her head was still spinning from all the door bashing and kissing, she thought back to the last conversation then had.

"You said you didn't need me."

"I don't need you, I want you." He leaned down and looked deep into her still watering eyes. "I want you more than I've ever wanted anything. Will you stay?"

Mary's heart quivered, barely able to beat from his admission.

Her brain, however, was a buzzkill of logic.

"Shouldn't you still be angry? Make me beg for your forgiveness a little?" This really seemed too easy.

George cleared his throat and took her hand, leading her to his bedroom.

"I saw you smash your phone from my window, that seemed like punishment enough."

His bed was large and covered with gray satin sheets. It seemed like the man just liked the color gray—she suddenly regretted complaining about it so much.

"And I can't pretend that I don't worship the

ground you walk on," he whispered into her ear. He was behind her, arms wrapped tenderly around her waist.

Mary just assumed George was playing along with her fantasy to gain sexual wisdom in a form that was comfortable for him. To believe that he truly saw her as someone worth worshiping was beyond anything she could have imagined.

Though, she supposed she had been imagining it in a way that was comfortable for her.

"Plus, I really am sad, lonely, virgin."

Mary moaned softly as he began nibbling the side of her neck. His tongue was skilled against her skin, he really had come a long way.

Sorrow crept into her chest as he continued to worship her neck with his mouth. Mary was good at many things, but hiding things was not one of them.

She was going to miss him.

Mary's moans became laced with tears which turned into sobs.

George detached from her neck and straightened.

"Woah, hey," His voice was gentle as he adjusted his grip to her shoulders and turned her to face him. "We don't have to," he cooed, concluding that she was having doubts about intercourse.

"No, I want to," she blubbered, tears and snot running together on her face. She attempted to wipe them away on the sleeve of her shirt, with moderate success.

"You're crying. What did I do?"

She laughed at how easily he took on her burdens.

He was so cute it made her cry harder.

There were no barriers between her and George, he had made her into an honest woman (and he had seen her have a phone-smashing breakdown so really it could only go up from here).

"I just don't want this to be over."

"But we haven't even started yet,"

"I'm scared you won't need me anymore," she explained, her fear clear between puffy eyelids. "Now you're so confident and your inbox is empty and-"

George's face relaxed in understanding.

"Oh, my sweet Mary," He clutched her tightly and threw his body onto the bed, smearing her tears on his shirt.

"As a beautiful woman once said to me in the library: you seem awfully worried about something that hasn't happened yet." His voice was so gentle and sweet, it made Mary hiccup.

"Did I ever say I needed your help with sex?" he asked.

Mary pondered for a moment, sniffling.

"Well, no, I guess not." She had assumed that experience would increase his confidence. Now that she thought about it he never even said he wanted to be more confident. Mary's assumptions really had made an ass out of her.

He took a deep breath.

"I've really messed this up, haven't I?" he mumbled to himself. Despite the fact that he was the one reassuring her, she couldn't let him believe any of this was his fault.

"No, I was-" she began to object, but was interrupted by his body weight rolling on top of hers. He braced his arms on either side of her head, pressing his face so close she could feel his breath on her lips. The weight and pressure of his body was comforting and slightly arousing.

"I don't need you to teach me how to have sex or manage my emails. I want those things. I want you, sweetheart. I love it when you order me around because I love you. I'm sorry I ever made you doubt that, I'll do better."

"Oh," Mary breathed, requiring a moment to collect herself. She had never even stopped to ponder that he began their relationship because she was inherently special to him.

She had stripped him of his agency, because of her stubborn self image. Now, due to her own silly insecurities she had ruined what could have been a magical night of sexual awakening.

She had to fix this.

He cleared his throat softly. "I don't want you to feel pressured but I would like it very much if you stayed." His length pressed against her, signaling his true intentions. Mary couldn't help but laugh.

Her prince was a true gentleman.

She pushed him to his back, settling herself on the stiff length with an involuntary grind of her hips.

"You're acting like it's my virginity and not yours," she joked, increasing the pressure on his groin. His eyebrows drew together in pleasure, eyes closing momentarily.

"To be fair you were crying," he groaned. She pulled down the waist of his pants, releasing the swollen erection from its prison.

It was already weeping for her, making a tingle of satisfaction and excitement bloom in Mary's core.

"You're right, I should be the one making you cry," she teased, stroking him slowly. He groaned softly when she twisted around the head, eyes still shut in pleasure.

This would not do at all.

"Look at me,"

He opened his eyes and propped up on his shoulders, watching her hand envelope his throbbing cock and work it to her pleasure. His breaths increased as she sped up, a thin layer of sweat covering his brow.

His cock twitched, signaling he was near release.

Mary's hand shifted from his aching member to the fabric of his shirt, lazily pulling the cotton upwards to reveal his abdomen and chest. Readjusting her thighs, she shimmied downwards and pressed a chaste kiss to the spot just above the head of his cock. It jumped, attempting to get her attention.

She ignored the needy length, instead choosing to nibble along the trail of hair that led to his bellybutton.

"Oh, god. I-I can't look or I'm going to-" he shuddered under the torturous pleasure of her tongue, the salty sweet flavour of his sweat was a delicious reminder of his suffering.

"Is it too much for you?"

He shut his eyes again and nodded.

"Should I give you a little break?"

He nodded again, the shaking of his head vigorous.

Her poor prince was barely hanging on.

She straightened and shuffled forward so his balls rested against her mons and his cock easily slid back into her hand. She didn't stroke, just gave the length a tight squeeze.

"I'm sorry your first time isn't more romantic, I didn't lay out any flower petals or anything."

"I'm allergic to most pollen," he gasped, her hand pumping him in agonizing slow strokes.

"Good to know. Do you want to come?" She stroked faster, relishing in the arch of his back as she did so.

"Y-yes, god, yes."

She continued working him at her leisure, watching in rapt attention as he writhed in sheer primal need to hold back the orgasm, to please his master.

He was beautiful, and he was hers.

She leaned forward to whisper in his ear, "You did such a good job holding on for me. Give me your come, now."

He did not hesitate, letting out a series of moans and painting her hand and his abdomen in hot, sticky, release.

When his cock ceased twitching, Mary stripped him of his shirt and used it to wipe them both, laying next to him with a satisfied sigh.

They laid there together for some time, and she took the opportunity to admire the planes of his face as he slowly came back from his high.

She examined his ivory skin, speckled with freckles and a light dusting of hair. His softening cock rested against his abdomen, braced on either side by prominent hip bones and pointing up towards a defined waist.

Her clit still throbbed with unreleased arousal, but she was content to just enjoy her George.

He rolled onto his side, facing her. Blue eyes roamed her body with a sleepy hunger, pausing at the cotton sleep shorts.

"May I?" he asked quietly, a hint of need returning to his gaze.

Mary nodded, her desire reawakened in earnest by his polite request.

It was George's night, and if he wanted to make her come, who was she to stop him?

He positioned himself between her thighs, carefully removing the fabric that covered her pussy.

Leaning into her core, he inhaled deeply. Mary bit back a moan, barely able keep her own eyes open as he began to feast. His tongue was hot and wet and licked her just the way she liked, alternating between sucking and nibbling on her clit.

He added one finger and then two, increasing her pleasure threefold. She began climbing up to the precipice quickly, her channel quivering before she was ready.

"Stop," she breathed. George immediately paused and withdrew his fingers, placing them in his mouth to clean off her arousal.

Mary closed her eyes, the image nearly forcing her off the cliff—soon he would be able to make her orgasm without even touching her.

George sat back on his haunches, waiting

for her order. She could make him do any-thing she wanted, whatever depraved and perverted fantasy she had, he would happi-ly fulfill.

It was a heady thought that certainly didn't make the throbbing between her legs ease.

And yet, all that Mary wanted to do at that moment, was make George happy.

"Are you ready to make love to me?" she asked, both to let him know that she was ready, and to make it clear that despite their power dynamic, this moment was his to dic-tate.

He nodded and stood, removing his pants before placing himself between her legs. He was already erect again, aroused by pleas-ing her.

Mary could have taken control and walked him through it, but she didn't need to.

She knew George and George knew her

body.

He needed to do this, to prove to himself more than her that he could do this well, that he could please her.

Slowly, he pressed himself against her entrance, hand trembling.

She propped up on her elbow and grasped his neck and waist, hoping the contact would strengthen him.

"That's it, baby," she cooed in his ear. "Make me feel good with your perfect fucking cock." She rested her forehead against his and watched as the bulbous head parted her folds.

He thrust in with one smooth movement, her pussy so slick he met no resistance.

Mary could not stifle the moan that poured from her mouth at the feeling of being filled by him at last. He silenced her with his lips, the force of his kiss pushing her flat on her back. He thrust again, with his cock and tongue, sending jolts of pleasure to her womb.

"Oh fuck," she groaned, gasping for air. "It's perfect, you're perfect."

His thrusts were steady and rhythmic, rubbing against her inside walls in just the right place. She needed more.

"For you," he panted into the crook of her neck. "It's for you."

She took one of his hands and placed it on her clit, rubbing his finger against her in the motion she needed.

His head snapped up, eyes locking with hers.

"Can you?"

"You can," she reassured, panting between words. She was already hovering on the precipice from his skillfully foreplay and magnificent cock, and only required a final push.

"Yes, I can. I can take care of you, I will take care of you." His eyes blazed as he pressed her clit and thrust rhythmically, determined to push them over the edge together. His words and fingers and cock were perfect and they were hers.

Her prince, her George, belonged only to Mary.

She threw her head back and screamed, her inner walls contracting around him, milking his release that she claimed as well. George let out a groan of his own and thrust into her with abandon, giving her pussy what it demanded.

He pulled her into his chest as he filled her, cries of pleasure muffled against the skin just above her breast.

She didn't know if he purposely chose the

place nearest to her heart to whisper sweet nothings into as he came down, but she supposed it didn't matter.

"I love you," she whispered after his breath had calmed and he had rolled off of her.

"I know," he said with a lazy smile. "I thought you could tell how much I loved you, but clearly I was wrong."

Mary idly traced his fingers as she laid on his chest, pondering how silly the entire situation was.

"Have you ever thought about programming a mind reading device? Would prevent a lot of misunderstandings."

"I never said I was a good programmer."

TO CLAIM A PRINCE

EPILOGUE

THREE MONTHS LATER

"I can't do it, I won't," the Prince mumbled into her bosom, hiding away from his problems. Mistress sighed and continued to stroke his hair.

Their time was over.

The Prince's wedding was scheduled in the morning, and he was embracing his Mistress, tucked into the safe confines of her arms and bed.

"You must," she said calmly. Mistress had grieved their eventual separation for several months, now resigned to loving her Prince from afar.

"Must I? I have siblings." Mistress snorted at his suggestion, the Prince only had an older sister and a young-er brother, neither of which were appropriate for the throne.

"You were born for this,"

"I was also born to love you." He lift-ed his head out of her cleavage to stare into dark reassuring eyes.

"How could I ever rule a kingdom when my queen is not beside me?" he pleaded, his voice full of anguish.

She gently gripped his chin, bringing his handsome face closer.

"The same as many kings before you. I do not need a title or a crown, when you look at me I feel as if I am your entire kingdom." A sweet kiss punctuated the declaration, though it did not have the desired effect.

The Prince groaned and rolled away from her, his bare chest facing the worn wood of the ceiling.

He was a magnificent sight, pants drifting low on prominent hips, revealing the top curls of his pubic hair.

Mistress had the sudden urge to run her fingers through it and tug.

"How can I be a husband to another woman when every part of me belongs to you?"

"Most royal marriages are not love matches." Mistress tucked herself into his chest, running a palm through the patch of hair below his navel.

"I would be expected to produce an heir." Despair rang clear in the Prince's voice.

The words morphed into knives of pain lodged in Mistress' gut.

"How am I to do that when my cock cannot even stand without your command?" He gestured towards the member in question.

"Really?" Mistress asked, amusement dancing in her eyes. He nodded meekly, flushed with embarrassment.

Looking down at the groin of his tailored trousers, Mistress had the sudden need to test his statement.

"I tried to pleasure myself, to prove

that I could perform when the time came," he explained, pulling out the soft member to demonstrate. "And yet, he laid there—useless and slumbering, offended I would even attempt such a thing." He shifted the sleeping cock from side to side.

Just as the Prince had predicted, he didn't even twitch.

Mistress giggled, surprised how much his cock's loyalty made her heart sing.

"He just needs a little motivation," she teased, removing the thin shift that obscured her flesh. The Prince's eyes roved her body hungrily.

Alas, his cock remained flaccid, waiting for command.

Mistress had to admit she was impressed. As much fun as this exploration was, admiring her Prince's goods had made her too needy.

Mistress straddled his abdomen, smearing her juices on the hard ridges of his abdominals.

The Prince moaned softly and placed his hands on her hips to aid her grinding.

"He better wake up, or his Mistress will be very disappointed," she threatened, pushing her clit against him. The pressure was delicious, but Mistress needed more.

The Prince pushed her pelvis down onto an already throbbing erection.

"Oh, good boy." She slipped him inside and sat, burying him to the hilt. The Prince let out a tortured groan.

"I'm afraid I won't last," he admitted, pistoning his hips roughly. He was so deep the thrusts settled in

Mistress' chest cavity, urging her to climax.

She reached forward and cradled his throat in her hand.

"You belong to me, even when you don't." His life was physically in her hand, just as hers had been in his for years.

"Even when we are apart, you will feel me here." Her hand squeezed the base of his neck.

His thrusts were feral, hitting her most pleasurable ridges.

"Yes, Mistress," he gasped, making her palm slip from its place. She came with a series of moans, drowning out his own sounds of release.

Eventually, she dismounted and lay beside him, admiring his sated form. Mistress didn't know what would happen tomorrow, and ultimately it was not up to her.

It was the Prince's choice.

"I trust you," she said, placing a palm over his heart.

"I will not disappoint you." he replied, placing a kiss on the back of her hand.

George was sitting on the couch.

His long fingers turned the page of the notebook, the red polished tips skirting across the paper. His gaze focused on the words of the page, delicate brows furrowed. His hair was messy, a stray section hanging in his line of vision. He paid it no attention, too engrossed in the story.

Her prince was truly beautiful.

Mary continued to admire him, acutely

aware of his movements. She did not miss when his breathing sped slightly, and she definitely did not miss his hand trailing up and wrapping around the side of his neck. A gentle palm pressed to the underside of his jaw, thumb resting on the lump in the center of his throat.

George let out a few shuddering breaths, a flush beginning to creep up his chest. Mary felt a twinge of heat to her sex.

"You want me to choke you," It wasn't a question because it didn't need to be.

He startled out of his fantasy, snapping his gaze to hers and lowering his hand back to the cushion.

He didn't reply but the flush on his cheeks was enough confirmation.

He tilted his head to the side, exposing his pale neck for her. She could see the subtle movements of his heartbeat beneath the skin, her mouth suddenly filled with saliva.

Mary accepted the silent invitation, seating herself on his lap, and tossing the notebook aside. She grabbed the hair at the nape of his neck and tilted his head backwards, causing his lips to part in surprised pleasure.

Her nose and lips skirted up the side of his neck, finishing centimeters from his ear.

"Why do you want it?" The back of his neck was slick with perspiration.

Was he aroused or ashamed?

She shifted her pelvis slightly, the hardness beneath her core letting her know the truth.

Definitely aroused.

"Did thinking about my hand on your throat make you hard?"

"Y-yes," he said, voice small and shaky.

"Why is that, pet? Are you curious about breath play?" she asked, tugging again on his hair. She placed a kiss just under his ear and shifted her hips once more.

"N-No," he answered, bucking upwards against her. The thin barrier of his pants did nothing dampen the shocks of pleasure caused by his bucking.

"Perhaps it's because I own you—your lips, your hands, your cock, and even your breath," she mused, nipping at his ear lobe.

A soft whimper was her reward, and it became clear what her prince needed.

She straightened and brought both hands to the nape of his neck. She pressed her thumbs gently on either side of his trachea.

His pleading gaze fixed to hers, begging for her touch, her pleasure. She leaned forward, their lips almost touching.

Carefully, she increased the pressure of her thumbs, ensuring that his breathing remained steady. Her hands were a cage around his most vital area, offering a brace of support but capable of great harm. She watched as the color of his face deepened and the focus of his eyes wavered. She released the pressure of her hands, and waited for the gasp of his breath.

He returned to her quickly, his cock twitching beneath her. The kiss she took from him was rough, echoing her desperation for the reassurance of his breaths in her mouth.

He mirrored her desperation, coaxing her tongue to dance with his.

"Please, may I touch you?" he pleaded. Her core pulsed in response, respirations increasing.

"Yes," she answered, desperate for the feel of his touch. She crashed their lips together again and buried her hands in his hair, wishing to inhale his essence into her lungs. His arms did not hesitate to wrap around her back, pressing her breasts to his chest. He could feel her rapid breaths against him, which spurred his sharp thrusts against her.

Shaking hands traveled down to the globes of her ass, guiding her hips in their grinding.

"Did you like it?" she breathed, yanking his head back to look at her.

"Yes," His eyes were steady but pleading.

"Why?" She purposely rubbed her pussy against the length of his shaft, noting the dampness left in her wake.

"B-because I'm yours,"

Her lips began to kiss and nip at his neck.

"Because you take such good care of me. You-you know what I need, and give me what I deserve. I never have to worry." He struggled to finish the sentence due to the pleasure of her ministrations.

"And what do you deserve right now?" she asked, nipping his neck harder. He shuddered beneath her.

"To make you come. Please, let me make you feel good." His bucking underneath her was wild, skin damp with the effort of restraint.

"Hmm, I don't think so, but I am in the mood for an orgasm. So, you are going to stay very still while I use my cock to get off. If you come without permission there will be consequences." She stood and removed her damp panties.

"Open,"

His mouth opened without hesitation, and she placed the ball of cloth inside. His jaw strained but his gaze remained steadfast.

Mary knew how much he loved this particular maneuver.

"Good boy," she smiled as his pupils darkened further.

She straddled his lap once more after extracting his erection from his pants. It was weeping at the tip, begging for her attention.

She felt sorry for the poor appendage, since she had no plans of doing so.

A quick stroke of her hand was rewarded with a tortured groan from her prince, his head thrown back. She removed his shirt, admiring the sleek contours of his chest. She gently stroked the light smattering of chest hair, noting that his torso was also damp with sweat.

Her poor pet was suffering for her.

A new rush of need filled her womb.

She pushed on his shoulders, leaning him back into the corner of the sectional. The crown of his cock massaged her inner labia, the notch of his head rubbing tenderly against her clit and weeping with every swipe.

He continued to moan with every pass, muffled by the cotton still stuffed in his mouth. Saliva ran down his chin, the vision causing Mary to speed up her efforts, arousal transforming to desperate need. She braced her arms on the couch above his head, increasing the pace of her work further.

Suddenly, she needed his eyes, needed his words. Mary ripped the panties from his mouth and tossed them across the room.

"Talk to me, pet," she demanded between shaking breaths.

"I-I don't know if I can," he breathed. "I'm trying so hard n-not to come. Your pussy is too hot and wet on me, and your tits are so close to my mouth. I'm drooling for you." he panted, the residue of saliva still on his face.

Mary gave the trail of spit a long lick, swallowing it down.

"Oh fuck, oh Jesus," he swore, shutting his eyes for a moment to collect himself.

Mary immediately stilled her movements. His eyes snapped open.

"Oh, no, no, please don't stop. I'm sorry, I won't look away," he promised, and Mary continued her grinding, although at a slower pace.

"My cock is drooling for you." He whimpered. "It needs your come. It's begging for it. I'm begging for it. Please,"

She could feel his balls tightening under her ass.

Her poor pet was trying so hard.

"You've been such a good boy, I think you've earned to come with your master. Would you like that?" she asked, tightening the movements of her clit.

"If it pleases you," he panted, barely able to push out the words. His whole body was shuddering, desperate for release.

Still, his need to please his master was stronger. Tears began to fill his eyes, his torment and conviction at war within them.

The friction compounded with his submission was too much for Mary to bear.

Lightning bolts of pleasure crawled up her body, fueling the contractions of her pussy. The sensation of her slick heat and pulsations took George's orgasm from him, despite his best efforts.

"Oh, fuck." He came with such force that the spurts of his release covered his abdomen and chest. Mary placed a soft kiss to his mouth, luxuriating in the softness of his lips and his devotion.

"You are such a good, good, boy," she whispered, and she meant every word.

Some time later Mary was laying on George's chest, enjoying the feel of his skin as he finished reading the latest entry in her notebook.

EPILOGUE

"How does the story end?" he asked, placing the book down once he finished. "Does he abdicate? Do they stay together in secret?"

Mary took a deep breath and hummed in pleasure.

Her post orgasm lethargy still lingered in her bones and tongue.

"I don't think it matters." She looked up into her prince's eyes, gazing down at her with adoration and devotion."They love each other, they'll figure it out."

She sighed and nuzzled into the crook of his arm, silently lamenting the conclusion of her imaginary love story (since it had jumped from the page and became her reality).

Though Mary had claimed her prince, she had a feeling deep inside that the story was far from over.

LOOKING FOR MORE?

KEEP READING FOR A SNEEK PEAK OF

TO FIND A PRINCESS

THE PRINCE SAGA: BOOK 2

CHAPTER 1
PRINCE MEETS WITCH

The swamp was dark, foul, and thoroughly committed to living up to every unpleasant stereotype about swamps.

The Prince's pampered nose recoiled from odors that belonged in night-mares rather than nature. He wad-ed through brown water, watching expensive leather boots accumulate layers of putrid sludge.

A week of scrubbing might restore

them to respectability—assuming they survived this harrowing adventure intact.

No point fretting about it. His Mistress would handle everything— she always took care of his needs and ensured he lived in the lap of luxury. Her supple curves and commanding voice flitted through his mind, a splash of comfort against the muck squelching between his toes.

His fingers found the golden necklace beneath his shirt, gripping the precious metal for reassurance. It originally belonged to his late mother, and he had wished to gift it to his queen— so she may see evidence of her beauty and the power she wielded over his heart. When he'd presented it, however, she'd refused with that maddeningly selfless shake of her head.

"It will be a scandal," she'd insisted, then demanded he wear it instead. "The whole world will be able to see it, but only we will know its significance. You will be able to feel its weight and remember that you are mine."

The memory of her hands fastening it around his neck still sent warmth through the Prince's chest. Even now, wading through foul water toward an uncertain fate, the weight of it against his skin whispered her faith in him. That warmth fueled him through the bog, validating this increasingly questionable decision.

He would think about his Mistress to get him through.

He would not think of the muck in his socks, and he would definitely stop gagging.

Mercifully, the ramshackle cottage

appeared quickly. The sound of his knuckles against the aged door mirrored the thumping of his heart hammering against the cage of his throat.

The Witch answered the door, smaller than he expected. She was not old, and not particularly ugly.

She also was not happy, which was the first predictable thing about her.

"I've paid my taxes." Arms crossed, she was a fortress preparing for siege.

"Wonderful to hear. May I come in?" The Prince's impatience leaked through attempted politeness. Her suspicious gaze lingered for a moment before she stepped aside with all the enthusiasm of someone inviting plague into their home. She had likely seen much of the plague, considering it was her the townspeople came to for healing.

Perhaps she could heal him of his heartbreak, as well.

Beyond the threshold, herbal scents saturated the air. Some pleasant, others distinctly ominous. The Prince wouldn't ponder what sinister spells those ingredients might serve, or whether the wall-mounted bottles contained flesh-dissolving substances.

One purpose had brought him here, and he would not forget it.

"I won't take much of your time." Mostly because the lingering swamp smell was a fist to his delicate stomach. "I simply need your help."

Her eyebrows shot up, then settled into skeptical furrows. "And why should I help you?"

Fair question, considering the Crown's track record with outcasts was a trail of broken promises. He collapsed into a cracked wooden chair, the furniture groaning under his weight.

"Don't you have pity for a heartbroken man?" He was to be married to a woman he didn't love while his Mistress suffered.

"No." she said flatly, settling in the chair across from him. "Men in love are pathetic creatures who hold no space in my heart."

It was most refreshing, her bluntness. Clearing his throat, the Prince persisted.

"What do you want? Money, land, a fancy title with its own hat?"

Her laugh was sharp and acidic. It was not the first time a royal sibling had offered her items of status, and time had not softened her to the idea. The Witch was not an evil woman, though perhaps slightly bitter at the circumstances she found herself in.

"I don't know if I can help you." Amusement danced in her dark eyes. "Since you haven't actually told me what you need."

"My Mistress." At her mention, his entire demeanor transformed. "I cannot fulfill my royal obligations because I need her as a man."

Something shifted in the Witch's expression. This particular anguish was an arrow to her heart, stirring sympathies she'd thought safely buried. His desperation was visible, though she could not yet understand what necessitated her involvement.

"Why not abdicate?"

A groan escaped him. He leaped up, restless energy driving him into agitated pacing.

"I know nothing else! Bred and raised for princedom, what useful skills could I offer her away from my throne? " Back and forth he paced, ignoring the floorboards' protests beneath his sopping boots. "Besides, she won't allow it. My obligation to the Kingdom trumps my obligation to love her, according to her philosophy."

The Witch's respect for this mysterious Mistress grew considerably. She understood such agony—swallowing personal desires for others' welfare. Golden hair and shy smiles were ghosts haunting her own memories, along with bitter knowledge of how quickly resentment poisoned even the purest love.

She rose and approached her herb collection with newfound purpose.

Loss was foreign territory to this Prince.

Real consequences for privileged choices?

Uncharted waters.

He didn't appreciate the effort genuine love required. His Mistress suffered identical failings—too frightened of failure and vulnerability. They were both stranded, joined in an equally distorted version of love, one ruled by fear.

The Witch knew at once how she could help this Prince in love.

Specific plants selected, she added them to the bubbling pot while weaving intention into each deliberate stir. A moment of doubt gripped her— it had been years since attempting this particular magic, and even then it had not been intentional.

The feeling passed quickly—love was the engine driving her actions, just as it was driving the Prince in his foolish (but admittedly honorable) quest.

"What will you do to become worthy?" She ladled the steaming brew into a ceramic mug.

"Anything. Everything." Sincerity was wildfire blazing in his eyes. She extended the cup in offering. Without hesitation, he accepted it, draining the contents in three determined swallows.

Dramatic smoke puffed, and when it cleared, only royal garments remained where the Prince had stood.

The Witch crouched down, momentarily panicked that she had made a miscalculation in her recipe. Relief flooded through her as movement stirred beneath silk—a sleek black cat emerged, blinking in obvious confusion at his dramatically altered perspec-

tive.

A golden chain hung loosely around the feline's shoulders—it must have been a necklace that had slipped free during the transformation, far too large for his diminished form. She retrieved it carefully, adjusting the chain to fit around his furry neck.

The Witch paused, a shot of grief at the recognition of the Queen's necklace. It reminded her of a different time, a different life, really. The precious metal that had once symbolized royal devotion now served as a simple collar—though even as a cat accessory, it remained absurdly ornate.

She gathered the transformed Prince into her arms and carried him to the front steps, gently setting him on the woven hemp doormat.

"Good luck, Prince." Farewell spoken, she closed the door with a soft click.

She bid him farewell and closed the wooden door with a soft click.

ABOUT THE AUTHOR

S. Nasonov is an independent romance author with a firm belief that everyone needs to relax.

She writes stories that allow men to relinquish their power, and simp unabashedly about women who are definitely overthinking the situation.

Her personal goal is to have you laughing on the first page and crying by the last.

She lives in a world where straight people don't exist and neither does normal. It's a neurodivergent realm, where nice guys finish first but sometimes don't finish at all.

When not writing she can be found chronically ill at large (so probably in bed, doomscrolling.)

If you have something to say about her book, she encourages the good, bad, and ugly. (She's just very bad at initiating conversations.)